The Irony Of True Love

Side Story

Leviel,

HOUSE OF TOBIT

ALEGNA EIRAM

The Irony Of True Love

Side Story

Leviel,

HOUSE OF TOBIT

# To John

Contents

Prologue

On that Monday afternoon, the scalding temperature felt a hundred degrees more than the weather forecast predicted. Sweat kept forming on Leviel's tanned face, no matter how she wiped it off.

One of the many miscalculations by the mortals, thought the young ersatz.

It mirrored the argument between Dr Errapel of Zywei Mole & Gen Research Lab and Terra Obi, a famous animal rights activist and environmentalist.

Leviel watched as they battled their points on the LED screen hanging on a skyscraper right across from where she sat.

A pity, the insightful debate went unnoticed—lost to a passerby.

The honking of vehicles on the busy square was loud enough to mute it and rock a man's brain. Others may not find it as hot. Its topic wasn't as juicy as a celebrity couple divorcing or a pop idol's next concert as she saw some figures pausing during the breaks. The world's physical condition was a mundane subject as long as it did not obstruct their daily lives. Or perhaps, should they bother to gaze up there, the flaming rays of the setting sun would obstruct their view of the gigantic screen and drawn to the riot of the peach and reddish-purple colours tinting the sky.

Leviel must admit that if so, she would not blame them.

Feeling the warmth seep through her pants from the steel frame she sat on, she popped into the creydon. Unlike the mortals whose weather changes by season, the creydon's temperature sticks with autumn.

As she relished the coolness, she observed the disparity of sombre grey structures below. It was a picturesque silhouette. But only for a moment.

As soon as the beauty faded, a dark patch covered the mouth of Naydene Delos Santos, the reporter mediating the discussion. It followed every movement of her mouth as if ripped from her face.

An annoyed fan was targeting her.

If one had a telescope or a supernatural sight, one could see the tiny golden-winged creature with two purple eyespots on its wings clinging to her face while its size adjusted to fit in sync with the display.

Leviel could not help chuckling as she settled atop the billboard frame. The hanging tarp, twice as large as the LED screen, shook and crumpled every time the eddies of wind passed. It made the woman stuck inside a cab across the river nervous.

Her agitation contrasted with Leviel's, whose legs dangled in the air while sitting on the edge. She twisted to her right and lay flat before tossing again. A minute passed before she found a comfortable position. She bent one knee and cushioned her head with her arm. Wanting to savour the respite from her duties, she closed her eyes.

"Add Cabernet Sauvignon, and you can count me in. Shall we say, in fifteen minutes?" The speaker was a woman in a grey tailored coat and tight skirt with a mobile phone on her ears. Her eyes darted from left to right as she crossed the street. "I'm just right at the corner of Sherbrook A."

The woman's remark earned a smirk from the young man behind her. "Women!"

Leviel's heartbeat stopped. Somehow, that single word invoked a sore on her chest, drawing her to pay more attention to him out of all the drones of babble she heard. Curious, she sailed down the street to get closer to him.

"Emmett!" said another young man with flaming orange hair, in ripped jeans and a tailored black coat, leaning on a post beside the street. Leviel wondered how he could afford to wear the coat despite the weather. He was waving his hand at Emmett, who reached the other side.

"Lopez, you've caught me. Lovely, just lovely." Emmett signalled a street vendor for two cigarette sticks, then bobbed at the ripped-jeans man.

Upon landing in the middle of the road, two prancing men walked straight into Leviel akin to air while she strode ahead, oblivious to the cars who passed through her. Her buttoned-down suit morphed into a black lacy dress and her pair of flat office shoes into three-inch stilettoes.

Without breaking her stride, she stepped from the creydon into the mortal world and reached Emmett, only to stumble as her heel hit a crack.

An arm supported her waist, and her eyes locked onto a pair of icy grey ones, dragging her thoughts into his. A series of sanguine sceneries invaded her vision, and for a moment, Leviel tasted a monster's craving for blood as if she was it. Then she changed to be an observer on the sidelines, revealing its true form. Suddenly, a clunk of wood hitting a triangle reverberated from the clouds, and the images vanished.

Emmett's arm slid off her as he flew like a steel tape measure, rolling backwards out of her reach before dissolving into smoke. When it cleared, a pair of dim, glassy eyes peered at her. Its owner was an old man garbed in rags. He was holding a paper cup while reaching up to passersby.

Nothing like a splash of cold water to rouse her from the spell. Leviel spotted the hole, and her brows knitted. She knew it wasn't there prior. But she lost her will to learn more before forming another thought as the triangle sound continued ringing. On instinct, she glanced at the skyscraper behind her.

A feather-like figure fell in a swift and landed atop a taxicab right when its female passenger, who felt uneasy about the billboard, exited.

The debris from the hood hit her head thereon.

Soon, a crowd formed, and traffic of vehicles ensued as curious mobs stopped to take a glimpse. But Leviel, heedless to the chaos, only stood, gritting her teeth while her eyes fixed on the corpse garbed in a bridal gown atop the cab.

Leviel reckoned her predicament was worse than the bleeding woman. So she didn't protest when two young men in a dark button-down suit flanked her sides and pulled her back to the creydon.

"You did this." The wind brought a man's hissing voice to Leviel's ears. None of the men beside her said it.

Leviel's insides shook as she watched one of the corpse's arms hanging at the driver's side. *Perhaps a struck of conscience.* If so, a first in this life.

Leviel hoped that one day, in another lifetime, the corpse's demise won't result from her handiwork.

Whom was she kidding? Leviel asked no one in particular as bitterness crept in. She's only an ersatz, unlike the dead girl.

A giant moth resting on the corpse's palm caught Leviel's eyes. It was identical to the blat in Naydene's mouth. When Leviel looked away, its eyespots drew her into a trance. Flashes of red and silver strings connecting one mortal to another flooded her mind before settling on the scene where white laces floated on a red aisle as a bride walked to the altar. Just as the bride reached for her groom's hand, the red string connecting them broke, and the groom asked the bride if she loved him.

"Stop!" Leviel shut her eyes, hoping it would go away, only for the scenes to be submerged by several episodes of a monster's killings.

A pair of golden scissors materialised. When Leviel stretched her arms, she only caught air.

Another triangle tingled, breaking her preoccupation.

When reality sunk in, she saw a burning light shooting down from the heavens, striking the cab's hood before a fiery being materialised, covering the corpse with fire.

Beaded sweats formed on Leviel's forehead as the shroud's temperature increased.

Leviel wasn't sure if it was because of the being's powers alone or the scorching glare he gave her before he beamed back to the heavens. Retribution. Leviel's sure it spelt of it.

"A pity you're one of us," said the man on her right, oblivious to Death's brief appearance.

The seraph would never show himself just to anyone. One must either owe the being or transgress against the seraph's wishes, like in Leviel's case.

"You couldn't wait after the 'I do's part.' You are indeed heartless," the ersatz from her left elbowed her.

Because Brianna should never marry whatever happens. It was the corpse's name. At least that's her name in this lifetime. But Leviel bit her tongue and refrained from saying it. She learned to elaborate on someone she would never see again was a waste. The ground quaked, as if confirming her thoughts.

A second later, its intensity increased, diverting the awkwardness.

Still, the three ersatzes stood frozen in place while they watched the city's structures crumble like a mountain of flour, scattering at the slightest touch. In less than a minute, what remains of what the mortal called their city was akin to fragments of chipped-off pieces of waffles.

With Leviel's dress replaced by her buttoned-down suit uniform, she vanished from the creydon with the others.

She appeared alone on an empty street in a blink, facing an ice-cloaked landscape while a blizzard grew thicker over the horizon. A gatehouse was close by. Attached to it was an arc walkway above the gates.

Three pale-looking blond men who wore the same uniform as Leviel's stood straight like statues on the bridge. Behind them was an enormous clock with a quarter of its face gone. It was bursting at a slow pace. With every step she took towards the gates, its long hand moved.

Leviel wondered how many lifetimes must she pass before half of it only remained? At the end of every lifetime, it looks the same to her. What if she dallied and waited, trapped in this in-between?

Black-golden wings came out behind the three figures, and Leviel vanquished the idea before they could read her mind.

"Faster, heartbreaker!" the figure at the centre barked. "Demons followed you."

Leviel teleported into the gates prior to his last statement and only then realised she had two shadows. It stretched to touch her, but the gates crashed into it.

"Show!" said the gatekeepers.

Several corpse-like creatures with elf ears and onyx glob eyes revealed themselves as they clung to the gates. They rattled the railings and crawled up to the bridge. But they kept slipping and falling, one after another.

Behind them, a thunderous boom of galloping hooves erupted. It sent them into a frenzy as a black knight emerged atop a racing horse. One demon flew back and fell, and the rest ended the same. But it didn't just stop there. While their shrieks amplified, they walked backwards on their own accord and pierced themselves at the sentinel's tilted lance until they all slid further down the pike, which now resembled a barbeque.

It wasn't the knight's doing; Leviel knew for certain. She glanced again at the backs of the figures atop the bridge. Then back to the voluntary slaughter. Their free will was nonexistent even before they touched the gates. Manipulation was a gatekeeper's most excellent skill.

"You best be on your way," said the figure in the middle.

Leviel could only nod; else, they might read her mind about how she finds them cruel most of the time. It was neither the time nor the place to challenge one of Gabrielle's angels.

As soon as she faced what remains of the clock, she burst into fragments of tiny pastel-coloured butterflies. They flew into the clock's focal point of explosion while it chimed as they wade in time. Not for long, the darkened passage faded, and the brilliant fields of yellow petals of canola welcomed Leviel, near blinding her sight.

Amid the blooming crucifers, she materialised at a rock with arms wide open, letting the wind kiss her face and blow her hair. Leviel watched as petals glided but could not sail too high before they burned and disappeared. Her absorption soon switched to her bronze arm devoid of red strings, young and bare, while her dull uniform was absent.

A fiery ball ignited above the clouds as if the sun had escaped its gravity.

Not long after, as it sensed her, the cool breeze turned into searing, the mountain backdrop and surrounding forest lit into flames akin to a current—painting the greens into black while the soot came in all directions.

Thousands of flying creatures fled to the heavens to escape.

Only Leviel remained unmoving, even though the flames were about to swallow her.

"Will you stop, Shiphrael?" Leviel asked, whose eyes were still at the burning ball above.

The howls of the other creatures were her only answer.

"Leviel!" came archangel Raphaelle's voice, but Leviel didn't even raise her head to her calling.

The fire soon took Leviel's legs. Still, she waited for Shiphrael.

"Did you? You reap what you sow, heartbreaker." A distant smirk came when the flames neared Leviel's shoulders. Then it swiftly took her and the mortal world. Except, Leviel's consciousness remained spiralling for a very long time before finding a mouth. A talking mouth. Then the riot of the peach, reddish-purple tinted sky, came to her view once more.

1

Greed

*W*eary cold eyes locked onto the purplish eyespots at the surface of a golden moth's hind wings as it landed at the thirteen-foot LED display atop a skyscraper. It hovered at the right shoulder of a woman with rimmed glasses. Her face was red as an apple.

"That is the point. Will this engineered organism you've studied save humanity or one at the expense of the rest?"

"Well, we shall see whether humanity indeed does care, as at present the condition of our environment only serves to prove men only care for his survival." Her opponent unbuttoned his stylish-breasted suit. "You may fight for it now. But when it threatens our very existence, I doubt you'll have the same stance. It doesn't matter the cost as long as the majority survives. That has always been innate to our DNA as animals. The rule of the jungle."

Their discussion blended with the honking vehicles on the busy square of Machado and lost to the crowd, but not Torriano. He could hear it as if he was there through the screen.

"Add cabernet sauvignon, and you can count me in. Shall we say, in fifteen minutes?" Torriano noticed a woman in a black tailored coat and tight skirt talking on her mobile phone while crossing the street. "I'm just right at the corner of Sherbrook A."

"Women!" said a young man heeling her, whose brows knitted. The said apartment was two buildings out. He shook his head as he walked ahead of the woman, meeting Torriano's pair of grey-teal sunken eyes, then looked away.

"Emmett!" called a man in ripped jeans and a dark coat with the sleeves rolled up to his elbows. Torriano had long noticed him, leaning on a post, observing passersby while drinking a cup of coffee. He dropped the paper cup into the trash bin and strolled to Emmett. Of course, it had to be empty by now, Torriano presumed. He'd been there long before the debate sizzled enough to match the weather.

"Lopez, you've caught me. Lovely, just lovely." Emmett swung to the vendor, a boy only fourteen years old. "Make it two." Emmett dropped some change at the boy's opened palm.

"Sure," said the vendor, who lit the cigarette sticks before handing them to Emmet. He then ceded the other to Lopez.

"Thanks, man. I near gave up on my caller." Lopez began sucking the cigarette.

"Oh?" Emmett gazed at the large screen, not interested in hearing what went on with Lopez's call.

Torriano assumed the young man wanted to be anywhere but with Lopez. Seeing the two together was a typical scene. From the corner of his eyes, the moth flew from the LED screen to the potted plant near Emmett. Its golden wings fluttered, appearing intrigued by what went on with Emmett's mind. Curious himself, Torriano read the young man's thoughts.

Emmett was there to take a break. He was neither there to reminisce on their job's craziness nor the office's clamorous noise.

"Well, there you have it, Dr Errapel, a renowned researcher on GM organisms. A billionaire and founder of the million-dollar foundation, Zywei Mole and Gen research lab. Thank you so much for your time." Naydene Delos Santos nodded to her guest and closed the debate, and it went on to a commercial break.

Torriano noticed Emmett's lips twitched as he read the word 'billionaire' on the subtitle.

Emmet doesn't know how many overtimes he must take to reach a tenth. Not that he believed there'll ever be a chance. Ridding off the negative thought, he darted his eyes from the screen and caught Torriano staring again. *Maybe it never left to begin with.*

Torriano made no reaction that the man was spot on in his espying him. Undaunted, he gave him a come hither look, daring Emmet to question him. But before Emmet could dwell on him, his attention moved to a woman in a dark lacy dress. One of her three-inch stiletto heels stuck on the pavement, and she toppled, grabbing Emmett's shirt.

Coincidence? Torriano does not think so. It was not part of the mundane scene.

He scanned the place, searching for the tiny creature, but it was nowhere in sight. Melancholy crept inside in its absence. Not wanting to unravel why, Torriano jerked his attention to the couple. The woman had regained her balance while Emmett's cigarette fell. He kept his eyes on the stick, regretting it had gone to waste. Oblivious to Emmett's mood, the woman pulled her leg to free the heel, stomping it twice to reassure herself it was still sturdy enough to walk on. Then, without a word, she left.

Emmett's eyes batted, as if he could not believe she had just deserted him without a thank you or an apology.

"It must be nice—" Lopez snickered.

"What?"

"—to have a pretty face."

Emmett blew a cloud of smoke at his face. "It was an accident." His ears were now red, and a touch of crimson crept over his face.

"Or by designed." Lopez threw the cigarette at a cup laid on the vendor's table. He glanced at his watch. "We got to go. The rush is upon—" But the sound of an alarm stifled his words.

Not a second later, dozens of workers from the tower construction behind them rushed out, meeting the hundreds of workers getting off work across the street.

Emmett and Lopez cursed in unison as they threaded through the throngs of workers. The mob swallowed their backs not a moment later, and Torriano could no longer distinguish them from the rest. Honks of cars and trucks stretched as the crowd ignored the traffic light. In a few minutes, the streets became congested, and none could walk without rubbing each other's shoulders.

Torriano gazed above when a fireball hit the tower's top at great speed. It disappeared in a blink while clouds gathered near the spire. Darkness wrapped the city in a moment. Not long after, lightning bolts struck, but none touched the mortals on the ground, to his dismay. As was typical, a downpour followed, making the masses below run in all directions. Almost everybody was busy with their troubles—finding a cover for themselves, crossing the busy street, or hailing a cab, especially as they tried to evade the splashes of water brought by the speeding cars, oblivious to the murky pool or the people it spattered on.

These made the crowd huddle closer to the building's wall. In a flash, people crammed like sardines on the sidewalks. None cared for Torriano in a withered raincoat that had seen better days who sat with his back on the wall. A weary, elderly woman was beside him. They were both shivering from the cold.

Despite being squeezed, he kept extending his arms to the stranded crowd. With each passing minute that these mortals ignored him, his teal-coloured eyes grew paler until only the grey remained, making him look frailer than he was.

"Say, how about we dash to the nearby pub?" A man in a rumpled shirt and tie appeared already hammered before tasting a drop of alcohol. He clamped his arm around his buddy. Both were standing next to Torriano, who now peered at them.

"Fifty. The reds won't even hit a goal tonight," said the buddy on a scarlet sweater. Compared to the other man, he was ten times more capital with his wet hair and shining face. But Torriano could find no drops on his clothing. It must be the hair jell or the damp weather.

"Two jars?" the rumpled guy asked, looking askance.

"Perfect."

When the two left, Torriano dropped his arm, laid the cup before him, and closed his eyes. Their conversation wasn't the only one that increased in volume in his head. He wanted nothing more than to follow them. If only a drink could help him.

The golden moth appeared once more. It flew past the mortal to the post light, and the noise in Torriano's head seized. He shut his eyes and only opened them once more when the rain stopped and the crowd dispersed. Torriano stayed motionless for hours until he saw a drunkard walking down the empty street, swaying as he neared him.

"You worked hard," said Uli, who grinned, grabbing Torriano's cup of coins and pouring the meagre sum into his palm before jamming them into his pockets. Torriano eyed the drunkard's movements: drew a cigarette and lighter from his pockets, covered one side near his mouth, and lit it. As soon as Uli dropped his hand, a punch landed on his face, and he stumbled. "You—" the drunkard swallowed the words he wanted to say as a familiar figure of Junior towered over him.

Junior is a namesake because he imitates their boss often. He's also the boss's right-hand man, befitting of its name, which meant his presence was neither a visit nor for pleasantries.

Now he's done for, Torriano thought. He took a step back and slid into his corner. Uli quivered while three of Junior's men surrounded him. At Junior's signal, they started beating him. Uli's screams echoed as he rolled onto his stomach and covered his head.

"So, it's why you have deposited less and less. Excellent!" Junior hunched over the drunk while his men stepped back. "You have been putting more in your pockets than the boss's coffers!" He sliced Uli's pockets, and Torriano's coins scattered.

One rolled to Torriano's foot, but he didn't move to pick it. He was more interested in Uli's helplessness as he peered between a pair of legs.

A black van honked and parked at the side of the street, alerting Junior's men. Two men dressed in known delivery company uniforms got out of the vehicle. "Elderly first!"

Several beggars under Uli's territory lined up near the van while one of Junior's men gestured to Torriano and the older woman napping at the side.

A long-awaited moment. But Torriano hid his excitement as Junior's man pulled him to his feet and roused the elderly. Without hesitation, they limped to the van in small steps. One of the delivery men ushered them inside, ahead of the others. Torriano took the seat at the rear, next to the windows and looked outside, fixed on Uli's head, but Junior moved, blocking his view.

One man grabbed Uli's arm and twisted it. His howls made the others within the van aghast, shivered and yelp, mirroring Uli's terror.

Preoccupied with Uli's troubles, no passenger noticed Torriano and the elderly merged into one and morphed into a hideous creature.

The only glimmer inside was from the post light. Suddenly, it dimmed, making the monster invisible. The delivery men collected more elderly and young children from the streets. Only when the doors refused to shut did they call it a day.

At midnight, the van reached the ports. They deposited their passengers into a container van, locking them in with the beast.

***

Junior turned his attention back to the matters in front of him. He waited for his men to finish collecting the coins and checking all of Junior's pockets before bending. "Do not trace the others and extort their collection," he whispered in Uli's ears. "Otherwise, this won't be the only thing you'll end up with."

Uli didn't have enough time to digest Junior's meaning because one thug rolled him, grabbed his arm, and twisted it.

"Ahh!" bawled Uli.

"I hope you learn your lesson. There are no second chances in our field," Junior dropped a dozen notes on Uli's heaving chest, appearing impassable. "Get yourself sorted, and Billy will pick you up in a week. You'll be working for Maddock going forward."

Uli wanted to plead his case, but the pain overwhelmed him, and he couldn't speak. Maddock was one of their outfit's distributors, famous for cutting his runners' fingers if they couldn't reach the number imposed. It was equivalent to a death sentence.

Junior flickered his fingers, and two of his men picked Uli while the other rolled the bills and slipped them into Uli's coat. "Till next week," said one thug, leaving him in an alley. The three marched to the waiting SUVs. "It's done, boss."

13

Junior gestured for them to get in. He turned up the car's stereo until it blasted pump-up music enough to blow their ears before they set off. They circled the city for a couple of hours before the convoy drove to the pier near midnight, where several men in a jumpsuit with a Ruger hanging on their shoulders stood at attention atop stacks of ship containers.

Junior's men got off with duffel bags not long after it parked. They unzipped the bags before lining up for inspection.

"The boss is upstairs. Go through, pronto," said Martin in his slick suit, looking distinguishable from the rest. He nodded at Junior before searching his men for weapons. Then gestured to the table where two women in uniform tailored suits counted the piles of bills and coins.

Their accountant, a grey-haired man, was busy tinkering on a laptop at the corner. He accepted the bags and threw them near the pile. "The usual?"

"I'll let one of my men get the receipt." Junior climbed the flight of stairs leading to the warehouse's office. Pausing at the entrance, he spun to survey the different hues of sea cans piled in the yard. Soon, this kingdom will be all his if his plan runs smooth. *Someday, not for long.* A man hiding behind his uniform was difficult to crush. *Though not impossible.*

"JUNIOR!" said Conrado, whose voice echoed in the warehouse. Impatience laced his voice.

The assistant shook his head and sighed. He masked his expression before he swung back to the open doors.

One guard stationed nodded at him. It was the head of Conrado's security, Lucas.

"Make sure they stay on their feet until the VIPs leave." Junior gestured for Lucas's men to get out. Lucas also followed them and closed the doors.

Junior spotted a dozen men in their late forties to fifties with bulging stomachs drinking with Conrado as he descended another flight of steps. He could see from their faces that their thirst for more coins was insatiable. It's why they get along very well.

"There you are, Junior. Come and help them which ones they should accept," said Conrado, who gestured to the open container van.

Junior stepped inside and dragged several young women dolled up in whatever predilections their guest preferred. He then introduced them to the VIPs.

Retro music, shouts of jeers, and maniacal laughs besieged the warehouse, masking the container's slight tossing near the accountant's table.

The jeering inside stopped a couple of hours later. So did the music. However, none went home.

The guards didn't find it unusual, so Lucas, who observed only a few guards remain standing, let another hour pass. Sleep tempted them the most. So fighting it off took priority over the yard they looked after.

Not a moment later, several piercing cries broke the silence. One guard fell from the container, stunned by it.

"What was that?" Martin shot off to his feet.

"Junior!" said Lucas over the radio.

Martin signalled for his men to rouse before pressing the radio. "Junior, come in!" With no response, he thumped at the container, gazing up when Lucas landed. "Anything?"

"Nothing. The radio's dead." Lucas panted and tried to catch his breath. He gestured to his men as he jumped off. "Come on!"

The howling from the warehouse grew and echoed to the shores, making them pause and sweat before carrying on. With Martin leading his men to open the main entrance, Lucas with his men went to the office stairs at the corner. They barged through with their rifles aimed, ready to shoot.

"Dammit!" Martin bumped into one of his soldiers. The guards at the front froze. "God, almighty!" Though his collywobbles made him believe he saw Wrath, not God.

A pool of sanguine liquid dominated the floor while a monstrous reptile-like creature dragged and bit the people within its reach. It chewed them into pieces, showering blood on the guards.

Lucas fired several shots but stopped when none made it to the beast. Over the gunshots, he tilted his shoulders and spoke to his radio, "WHERE ARE CONRADO AND the VIPs?"

"Gone," said Martin over the radio.

Soon, it struck the rest that their weapon was useless. An invisible veil covered the monster. When the men ran out of bullets, the guards dropped their firearms with their mouths agape, only to reload, point and fire again.

"You are resilient when hope is all lost," said a deep man's voice. It took them a while to realise it was the beast. It circled them before it disappeared.

Martin and Lucas's men came together at the centre.

"Not a single body!"

"Leave!"

"Let's go!"

The men scrambled in unison as they tried to run, but their legs wouldn't obey.

"What's going on?"

"No. Oh please, no!"

"What the bloody—"

A sudden hissing sound near the guards' ears appeared, but no creature was beside them, and they lost their voice. Silver-teal eyes watched as their knees quivered, almost in tune with the rapid pounding of their heart as it continued in circles, extending their dread.

Meanwhile, a ship's siren from a distance broke their preoccupation. The hissing noise vanished. Several minutes ticked by when Junior's head rolled towards them out of the blue, breaking their respite. One even fainted.

A long, gigantic tongue wrapped them all in a swift, leaving them no time to ponder. Squeezed together, their bones broke, and their blood splattered on the ground, adding to the thick gooey slime from the monster's saliva. Then it chewed their mangled body, relishing their cries of pain.

****

A power outage befell the city at four in the morning, shrouding the place in darkness. The foul smell of a rotten dead rat and several days old blood stretched to the shores, sending authorities to investigate, but none could trace a corpse or a single drop of blood.

"Ich fühle mich aufgebläht," came a deep voice from the heavens. Then a lightning bolt followed, landing at a stack of a shipping container. A child with a luminous body materialised and surveyed the yard before focusing on the grey-eyed monster he could see through the walls.

"Excellent!" said the child, while he clapped with glee. He vanished and reappeared in a blink within the warehouse. Taken aback, the monster swallowed the bulk he had not chewed enough.

"Slow. I will not ask for a share," said the child in amusement. However, the monster lost his appetite and spat out three arms before transforming into a man's figure. The limbs on the ground rotted until none were visible.

He approached the child, paused, and bobbed. A metallic mask appeared, and he covered his face, revealing only a fourth. But his gleaming silver-teal eyes transformed into a dead onyx bead. Without preamble, he stepped back until darkness consumed him.

The child morphed into a raven-haired girl wearing stiletto-heeled shoes. Her laughter sent icy shivers to anyone who could hear her. From the corner of her eyes, she watched as the moth flew into her palm.

"You are braver than I gave you credit for."

She held the puny winged creature and examined it before her eyes. "One is a monster, and the other is a delicate insect at my mercy." Then her palm closed to crash it, only to find it gone. She laughed once more before a veil of fire cloaked her. When it dissolved into smoke, it revealed a cherub with a burgundy gem on its forehead.

2

Calling it off

Around the end of September, multiple chestnut-shaded moths with rimmed pink eyespots on their wings materialised at the nixie world's entrance, arranged like a spine. One of the giant terracotta twin guardian frogs, Liebman, darted its tongue to stop them. But it was less than a second too late, and they flew in helter-skelter. He knew full well that his body was no match for its speed. So he used telepathy to chase them.

After a while, he found himself outside the Khycen castle, where two twenty-foot golden dragons emitting toxins sat at the tower. He knew they weren't real, for he'd never seen them move. But the moths passed the poisonous barrier without delay and barged through the keep. Liebman had no choice, so he willed himself to trespass on the ersatz grounds.

Not a moment later, he arrived at a golden chamber decorated with floral wallpapers. The moths swoop into a girl's forehead, asleep on a queen-sized bed. Liebman's tongue sprung but caught a few of the girl's hair bangs instead.

"Ahh!" yelped Leviel as he wiped away the saliva from her face, making Liebman still. He was very much afraid of Lord Khycen's only daughter. Being reborn too many times only brings bad luck. And so unlike the other ersatz of her kind. She doesn't seem to fit in with the rest of the cupids. But as a warrior, she was the best among the rest. Even only as a nursling.

Liebman stepped into the creydon, a sphere a mortal could not see with their naked eye, hoping Leviel would not notice him. Here, different beings like the dead, Nephilim, demons, and the likes roam. Only a mortal who possessed a third eye could see this sphere.

Leviel thumped on to her pillows. "LEIBMAN. Come out!"

Filled with dread, Liebman used his front legs to cover his face. But his quivering hind legs could not support his weight and tumbled. His body came out of the creydon and crashed onto the bedside table, rocking the porcelain vase off. The entire bedroom lit as soon as it fell while Leviel's eyes veered in his direction, meeting his half-moon dark eyes.

Liebman recovered first. He jumped off right into the window. The magical world created to shelter thousands of mystical creatures such as the trolls, fairies, elves, and the likes welcomed him.

Leviel ran after him into her balcony, took off one of her slippers and slung it to the frog hopping midway to the footbridge. He fell into the lake.

As she waited for Liebman to resurface, the dusk outside made her pause. At least it was dusk now in the mortal world. Leviel doesn't know what they call it there. Remembering to appreciate being back from the dead, she calmed. But unlike her other lifetime, Thomas never visited to bestow on her the golden scissors he always did on her fifteenth birthday. Mayhap because now she's the only heir, Leviel assumed. She's been stuck in the nixie world longer than she expected.

In the mortal world, one sees a shopping mall occupying twenty blocks on the side of an avenue. But within the nixie world, a massive mangrove forest covers this space. Here, greenish-blue, dark thick arms of trees support several huts with steep slope roofs and round terraces akin to a teacup in a saucer. Mortal-like creatures with wings instead of limbs dwell in these tiny houses. Smooth marbled water below reflected the trees' boughs.

Across this, instead of a stadium, lies an enormous forest with trees bearing monstrous roseate leaves and burgundy spotted mushrooms.

Perched on its branches are gigantic amber-coloured puffy sparrows. Only their eyes moved and followed the flapping wings of the golden-blue and white kingfisher. Flocks of them swirled to the canopy, wanting to escape its foliage. Their cries were the only disturbance.

One can mistake this for a fairyland. But fairies aside, it is the sanctuary of the witches—the select few.

It's also the home of the ersatz's head—the Khycen clan. Since they were mortals turned angels, the fairies consider them as their royal family despite not sharing a single DNA.

"Aaah!" came Liebman's shrieks as he slipped back into the water. The loud splash near emptied the lake. Most creatures in this world are twenty times larger than the mortals. Liebman rose his head but hid half of it in the water and darted his eyes to her balcony. "I only wanted to stop the moths, my lady."

The giant frog cursed when a force drew him out of the water and shoved him to the bank.

Moths.

It elicited a vision while Leviel's eyes gleamed.

She didn't know why she kept dreaming about the monster and the child. Once, she saw her eyes on it, while in its mortal form. That was several dreams before becoming the monster's companion child, similar to what she dreamed before Liebman licked her face.

The alarm she set the night earlier rang, making her run inside to her bedside and glare at it. It never rang before she woke.

Leviel grabbed the device, hid it in the drawer on her bedside table, and then lay back on her bed. She stared at the empty ceiling and then closed her eyes. The monster's lifeless eyes unfolded, making her roll to her side, facing her five-foot cabinet mirror where the greys in her light blue eyes accentuated akin to the monster's.

"Vorsichtig!" came a shout outside, making Leviel leap off the bed.

The sun appeared to have risen. Leviel discovered the studio lights installed outside were on. She drew out the alarm clock. It was five past seven in the morning.

A loud banging and screeching sound made her run back to the balcony, where she saw several of her mother's aides arranging flowers on the grounds. Now chairs and laces dominated the bare courtyard.

"If you're awake, have Bona help you," said her mother in her head. Bona is her mother's secretary.

Leviel bit her tongue to stop herself from retorting. She hated it when her mother used telepathy to check on her. She has yet to master shutting her out of her mind.

Despite that, Leviel followed her instructions, grabbed her robe, and stepped out of her room. As she tied the belt, her dream's debate flashed in her mind again. Her last night's dream made her notice the date. It was only a year ago. She only caught on to it now. That, and Briana died first before Shiphrael awoke.

Collywobbles crept down the pit of her stomach.

"Good morning, my lady."

Leviel glanced up and found Bona standing across from her with several women pushing three racks of frocks behind her. They paused and waited for Leviel's command. At least they were the only ones from her entourage on her floor. Leviel espied the rest through the slits of the bannister. The line stretched down to the bottom of the stairs. For an ersatz, they appear to rely more on staffing.

"Give me a second." She left them through a second stair leading to the administration wing of the castle and headed to her father's study.

When she strode inside, Foniel, her father's assistant, was on his feet and greeted her. Without breaking her pace, she nodded. "I need to use your computer for a second," she strode in without Foliel's acquiescent. Leviel sat in his chair and opened his laptop. She typed in Zywei Mole and Gen research lab in a search browser. Nothing came back. So, she keyed in 'Dr Errapel, geneticist'. Still, nothing came with anything reliable.

"Is there something I can help with?" Lord Khycen asked, who paused just outside the door frame.

Leviel peeked from the laptop's screen and found her father in an impeccable black classic fit suit. "There's one. Have you heard of Zywei Mole and Gen research lab?"

Lord Khycen's brows knitted as he strolled and motioned for his assistant to step out.

Foliel went as bided.

"Yes, I have." Lord Khycen rubbed his hands. "However, it's your engagement day. It is not the time for this."

Leviel gave him an irked look. "I'm only eighteen. There are still plenty of—"

"If you mean an ersatz who is interested in marrying into our family? Then you are mistaken. Few will jump into the boiling oil." Lord Khycen raised his hand before she could launch into a tirade.

Leviel believes that since it's already the 20th century, parents no longer may arrange their children's lives without their consent.

"Who is Dr Errapel?"

"And we're back at that again." His grey eyes grew cloudy and then cleared. It didn't escape Leviel's notice.

"Are you working with him?" Leviel asked, not wanting to cede until her father gave her an answer.

"His background is questionable," Lord Khycen grumbled as he jammed his hands on his trousers pockets, gave her an exasperated look and took a seat at one of the visitor's chairs facing the office table. "I have not concluded if he fights alongside the Grigori or us. Is this about your dreams again?"

Leviel once shared it with her parents, for she thought they could shed light on it and point at one or two valuable courses of action to address her visions. Her mother descended from the most powerful seer. She knew not to ignore it. To Leviel's dismay, they were dismissive. So she has never tried to mention it again. *Well, until now.*

Disheartened, she bobbed her head while opening a different browser. After the results came up, she shifted the laptop to face him. "I want to enter Galen."

Lord Khycen paled, then brightened. "Blimey! Your mother will be very disappointed."

Anything that annoys the archangel of death gets his approval right away.

"Gutted, but it's my life." Amusement etched on her face. Lord Khycen rolled his eyes at that, stopping himself from reproaching her.

Although the Khycen clan has been at odds with Thanatos Galen for a millennium, he can't stop an ersatz from entering his school.

The story says Azrael himself escorted Lord Khycen's grandfather to the middle, only to be intercepted by Raphaelle.

Michael's mightiest general gave him her blood, which allowed his descendants to be a conduit of her powers. It was his children that served as Raphaelle's Knights.

"We parent only wish the best for our children," he said, who still couldn't hold himself back from rebutting.

The left corner of Leviel's mouth twitched. "Right. For the good of our bloodline."

"That is unavoidable." Lord Khycen crossed his arms over his chest and leaned back in his chair. "Oh, well, let me be the bearer of bad news."

"Thank you. I supposed," said Leviel, not knowing if her father took this seriously.

"No need. A husband must take care of his wife's fury. Though you should stir clear before and after the eruption." He rose from the chair and tapped her head as he swerved, heading to the door. "I can only shield you in this matter. I'm afraid the rest is up to you."

Leviel beamed. Then squinted her eyes. "Are you certain?"

"You're not?" He dared her to cower. Lost for words, she only blinked. He didn't care and strode out.

Leviel only saw the door shut as it dawned on her—she didn't even have the chance to show him her gratitude.

Not a moment later, she heard Bona greet him in the corridor.

"And where is Lady Leviel?"

Leviel dashed to the doors to peer at them, then glanced at her night robes and winced. She should have thought about everything before dropping it on her father. Her father was a firm believer in proper planning.

"Sir, what do you mean?" she heard Bona ask, whose tone rose but not loud enough to be a shout.

Leviel knew it was about to go smelting and locked the doors. She then took the next obvious exit—the windows. But hesitated as she looked below.

Why was it several feet above the ground? Did her father move his study, or was it because she was desperate that she forgot?

The voices in the corridor climbed, making her even more determined. So Leviel closed her eyes and willed herself to teleport. Except she spiralled and lost control.

An arm caught her in a flash. A young man in a tux with red curly locks settled her on her feet. "A door is always an option."

Leviel grimaced as she arranged her clothing. "Oh! Hello, Seveeniel. Not with mother on the verge—"

"LEVIEL!" Her mother's roar echoed above, cutting her words and sending the droves of servants to rush back into the keep.

"O-Oh," said the young man. He pulled a button and handed it to her. "You might need this." Leviel only eyed it. "Your locket, which my father designed," he pointed at her necklace, "can project a thirty-inch shield once you insert a film into it."

Leviel's eyes rounded, and she grabbed the button. "Your dad's the best. Thanks!"

"You're welcome," said Seveeniel, bobbing his head.

Leviel turned to leave but felt she missed an important detail. Then he remembered why he was at the castle grounds. "Sorry about the engagement." Her face burned in an instant. But knew contriteness wasn't enough to compensate for losing his family's face.

He gave her a forced smile and said, "I saw it coming. It's all for the best." Seveeniel shrugged his shoulders as if it was all right.

"Will you not wait for me?"

Leviel needed to make sure she could indeed leave without a care. She didn't want to be startled later at finding their engagement still holds. Leviel knew it was too much. She did just pull the rug from beneath him.

"Time will tell."

His smiles disappeared, surprising her, and she thought of him as odd. He looked like a puppy she discarded. Seveeniel and his family were eager to have an affinity with the Khycen clan. She wasn't aware of his feelings of anything other than the mutual benefit they could reap from this engagement. Perhaps she would have found him interesting if he had been this way earlier. Now, she didn't have time to bother with him.

***

The corner of Seveeniel's mouth lifted as he watched her leaving. She raised one of her arms and disappeared with one of the golden dragons atop the tower.

"Til we meet again, heartbreaker." It's a promise. Seveeniel stared at the dark sky through the canopy's opening. He then morphed into a monstrous lizard and leapt into a bush.

One of the beast's forelimbs stomped on a young man's body with red curly hair locks in a black and white tux. Liquid dripped from its mouth as it pondered whether to eat the young man. However, since it took its time, the tower bell chimed. Disappointed, its tongue took the bouquet of tulips and gobbled it.

After swallowing it, the creature morphed into its mortal form. The man covered his face with a silver mask, with only his teal gleaming eyes visible. Then the studio lights dimmed, and darkness took the silver masked monster.

3

Exiting Nixie

As daylight began, bleak hints of apricots mixed in with the blues appeared on the horizon. A horde of monstrous flying creatures broke free from the creydon. Behind their backs were mortal-like young adults. The most unusual of the flock was a giant white horse-like beast with a golden plaque on its forehead leading them. A thick fur covered its neck and chest without a rider.

While mortals enter Galen via an aeroplane, ersatzes do so in this fashion. Youngling ersatzes weren't adept at flying or teleporting at this phase and therefore relied on their pets to get them there. Not so much for a celestial angel. They were well adept at flying since their nursling age.

It seems easier to pop up at the uni grounds. But since the humans would bring an outsider, they'd have to keep their true form hidden until Galen is sure they've rid them.

At seven sharp, they halted near the edge of a cliff seventy-two miles from the city—the ersatz version of an airport.

Leviel, in a one-off shoulder short sepia dress, alighted from her golden-white dragon with a fernlike tail. A dozen eyes fixed on her.

"Is that her?"

"Who?"

"The last of the true blood ersatz?"

"Leviel—THE LADY Khycen?"

"Hush! She can hear you."

Leviel peered at the group, huddled at the sides, craning to inspect her. She returned her attention to her dragon, only to glance back. She saw the jerseys they had on and turned her dress into her running attire.

With another pat and hug, Leviel raised her arms, and her dragon dematerialised. Then she braced herself as she faced the crowd's curious stares. Some welcomed her with a smile or a nod. Leviel returned it, although she knew none of them. Others, who felt ashamed, averted their gazes. Of course, their surprised reaction was only natural by her sudden arrival. Not even the Selkirks, the other ersatz family with Rapahelle's blood, and her close cousins were aware of her attendance.

Since they were still a few miles away from the city, Leviel presumed they awaited their ride—not just to gawk at her. She scanned the meadow and saw hers nearby. Relieved, she boarded a number seven coaster bus without glancing at the others.

A grey-haired lady with crestfallen eyes marched to her. She stretched her right arm for a handshake. "Welcome to Galen. I'm Zillah. You can call me Mrs Z."

Leviel shook the woman's hand, knowing what those looks meant. *Sympathy.* "Glad to meet you. I'm Leviel."

"Your father and I spoke. I carried out his arrangements for you ahead of time." Mrs Z gestured for her to sit down.

"Thank you."

Leviel took the nearest seat to her left, and they set off straight away. She observed Mrs Z, and the driver wasn't keen on chatting with her, which suited her mood.

The scenery they passed was ordinary, for she knew the route to the university from memory. At finding nothing to interest her, the ride lulled her to sleep in the next moments.

A sound of a helicopter taking off roused her. Leviel sensed there were more people alighted on the coaster bus.

"It's hot in here." A woman slammed the windows open. "Galen could at least offer the same accommodation as they did at the airport."

They welcomed us with a Bentley. Why can't they do so now? The coaster bus was the worst downgrade of rides they have ever picked.

Leviel smirked at hearing what the mortal didn't dare to voice. Curious, she glanced at the griper—a sandy-haired woman in a pink suit spoke to a blonde girl of Leviel's age. Her dress matched the tone of the older woman's attire—tailored to their size by the looks of it.

The girl looked embarrassed and gaped at Leviel. She gave her a lopsided grin.

Leviel didn't shy from her and carried on staring.

Discomfited, the girl touched her hair and then approached Leviel. "Hi, I'm Tirzah. Forgive me-er-she is my mother." She pointed at the woman on her right, who peered at Leviel. Then back to giving Mrs Z a sour face. The latter was now apologising for Galen's 'downgraded ride.'

Tirzah narrowed her eyes at her mother and then jerked to Leviel. "We're not used to waiting in a coaster. And—well, she's high strung. Do excuse us."

"Indeed. I had never ridden a bus before either." Leviel darted her eyes to Tirzah's mother. "As the rest of us." Tirzah's mother paused mid-sentence as she spoke to Mrs Z. Leviel hid a grin and shook Tirzah's hand. "Call me Leviel."

"What goodies in the basket did you get during your Bentley ride?" Tirzah asked, who sat down, beaming, filled with interest.

"I didn't. There was no Bentley for our kind."

Tirzah's eyes batted for a while, trying to absorb what she heard. The pounding of her heart increased by the second. "I thought they won't at least mix us," she lowered her voice.

"Only the Houses-er-headquarters," Leviel pointed at the folder Tirzah held. It has Galen's logo on it and Tirzah's name. "Our lodging is a different matter—I'm sure it's on one of those papers in your folders. Do try to read them."

And with that statement, Tirzah joined back her mother and Mrs Z's conversation.

When silence reigned several minutes later, Leviel felt relaxed. She leaned her head on the window and went back to napping. But after half an hour, more students clambered aboard the vehicle.

Leviel roused, feeling vexed. She fastened her eyes on the clearing, counting down, beginning at one thousand.

"Aren't we all set to go?" Tirzah's mother asked, eliciting a grunt from Leviel.

"We're waiting for one more," said Mrs Z, giving Leviel half a smile before getting off.

A loud banging on the bus steps came at the open door. Leviel saw a girl with thin arms. Her head bowed while pulling a suitcase. It kept slipping back to the ground because its wheels could only reach the edge of the steps before gravity drew it back.

Mortal, Leviel assumed.

If no outsiders were present, she could help without lifting a finger.

"You must be Absolute. We're going to be roommates," Tirzah called out to the latecomer with glee.

Good, Leviel thought, she'd helped. But Tirzah only kept sitting and smiling as she chattered. *Gosh, it must hurt smiling for hours.*

The new arrival attempted once more, and the banging resumed. Leviel could no longer stand the noise, and before Tirzah's mother became more upset than she was, Leviel approached the girl to give her a helping hand.

"I'm Leviel," she grabbed the handle of the girl's suitcase.

"Thanks," said Absolute, facing her.

Shit! Leviel near dropped the luggage.

"Sybil," said another girl—a witch. Then pointed to someone seated at the front. "She's Dove."

When Leviel recovered from her shock, she left them with their introductions. She got off the bus and carried the rest of Absolute's suitcases aboard. Then deposited them beside an older woman who came with the girl. Perhaps her mother.

Leviel returned to her seat and calmed her racing mind by averting her gaze outside. A line of limousines drove on the strip to fetch the newcomers. Others notice it, too. Now there was no way to stop Tirzah's mother from exploding.

"LOOK AT THAT—"

"Mother!" Tirzah warned her.

Sybil ran to the empty seat in front of Leviel's and plastered her face on the window. "That must be Lady Shuruppak."

Tirzah dashed to Sybil's side, ignoring her mother's dark face. "Is she a royalty or a peer?"

"Not your royalty." Sybil glanced at Tirzah and then jerked her head back to the windows.

"Around here, she is," said the nerdy mortal girl, Dove. She set aside the book she was reading before joining the others.

"Of course," said Tirzah's mother, who deemed it the only acceptable explanation for Galen's slight.

"Girls, settle down," came Mrs Z's voice as she lighted the bus. She began orienting them on their schedule for today.

Leviel stared at Mrs Z's lips as she spoke but blocked her words and the rest of the noise.

> *A white, glowing figure unfolded in her consciousness. It was of a girl whose face cringed in agony. Then the scene transformed into a basilica burning at Galen's grounds while a horde of ersatzes, mortals and angels lay dead. The girl stood at the centre with blue and scarlet blood on her feet. Leviel reached out to touch her.*

The visions disappeared in a blink.

My lady, take care of yourself, said Leviel's dragon into her head.

You do the same.

Leviel espied the large trees lined up at the sides of the road while squeezing the locket on her necklace. She opened the latch and stared at the watch within. It was the miniature version of the gigantic clock guarded by the gatekeepers. Only it stopped working at six o'clock. Leviel pressed the knob at the sides, and the hands moved.

At last, I arrived.

4

Ruined Manor

Leviel spent the quick tour Mrs Z conducted, observing the mortal-like students, trying to hide their true form. She felt pity for them—doing their best to accommodate the mortals.

Given that Galen was neutral ground, the creydon does not exist there. Its absence was more for the mortal's security. Hence, the ersatzes entrance from the nixie world was at the cliff.

Humans aside, most of these unearthly creatures weren't there to study. They were there as delegates of their race or a front to spy. If Leviel's vision proves correct, then it is only logical. Every race would weigh the winner of the pending war.

After their quick lunch at Délicieux Plat, a posh dining bar outside the uni grounds, which was indeed repas délicieux, the bus drove into a compound of neatly built mansions. Leviel's face brightened, and she grinned at the landscape. It only meant they didn't have to share a cramped room. It wouldn't bode well for her plans if she shared a room with anyone. And for certain, the rest shared the same sentiment.

When the others alighted, and only Mrs Z lingered, Leviel removed her phoenix engraved silver armband. It was visible only to her. She pulled a tiny trunk underneath her chair where a map lay inside. The near-torn yellowish map morphed into a small button and flew into her locket. She then replaced it with her armband and returned the box to its place.

Leviel stepped out of the vehicle and followed the rest to the manor. When she reached its main doors, it swung open on its own. She tried to take everything at once. Above the tented ceiling, near eleven feet high—three layers of chandelier hung from the beam of the glass roof. Chatters echoed through the sheer size of the space.

"Leviel?" called Mrs Z, who was at the second-floor gallery, craning over the balustrade. "The first door on the right." Mrs Z gestured to the opposite wing from where she stood. "We're heading back to the school ground in a couple of hours, so keep it short. You have the rest of the school year to get acquainted with the manor."

"Perfect." Leviel hid her grin while climbing the stairs and went to her room.

A golden chest appeared in her hands. With her powers, she found a hollow space behind the wall where a red velvet winged chair parked. It was near the manor's pillar. She waved, and the chair slid to the side. The chest flew into the wall without making a hole. The chair slid back to its original position.

Leviel checked the bath and toilet and then strode to the walk-in closet. Inside were her frocks, hanging on the racks, while folded casual wear laid on the shelves arranged by colours.

It was all thanks to her father's staff members. His attendants do things without delay. It doesn't seem bad now, coming there without her parents. She'd been to Galen several times before, but it was always with an aide or one of her family members. Her duty to Raphaelle's division always began on her fifteenth birthday, and Thomas reserved a suite only for her at Tobit.

The clock on the wall neared one in the afternoon, stirring her to move. *No time to dally, it seems.*

She strode to the door and peeked into the hallway. Gone were the incessant chatters. They must be at rest or preoccupied with familiarising themselves with their room, Leviel assumed. She barred the door, changed into a dark dress, and paired it with her black boots. Then grabbed her side pack before dashing to the parked coaster bus.

As soon as she boarded, she scanned the vehicle frame using her powers. When she was sure she was alone, Leviel settled in the back seat and willed herself to sleep. She activated her doppelt mode, and her body duplicated in less than a second. Leviel's original body left while her clone napped without care.

She inherited her father's ability to be in three places at once. It was rare for an ersatz to have such powers. So far, within their bloodline, only Leviel and her father have it. Whilst only a few favoured archangels and seraph do. They took on a proxy, which is a mortal form. But it does not resemble their angelic figure, despite the power it wields. Only Gabrielle could do four at once. And never with a proxy. That makes her one of the most formidable archangels among Michael's cadre.

Leviel materialised in a dark forest, where the temperature felt the exact opposite of Galen's.

Mayhap around negative.

She spotted a clearing through the slits of trees and the shiny ebony eyes of a red deer that paused and peered at her. The next instant, she stood beside it, where they appeared in a stalemate. Then it trotted off to the foot of a mountain.

She found it awaiting her near a series of steps leading to a cave. But as she drew near, it set off again. That stop, however, made her take notice of the ruined construction to her right. Her mind assembled what it was prior, making Leviel startled. It was a castle's keep for elves.

No doubt one guarded the place then.

She skimmed through the cave's opening, and upon closer inspection, it was a passage.

Leviel teleported herself to the opposite end and found a withered garden with a run-down fountain and further steps leading to a broken bridge. The deer stood atop mid-air at the missing part of the bridge. It kept slamming its head to an invisible wall, eliciting a thud.

Leviel's brows drew together. At lightning speed, she stood beside it. The deer peered at her. Then moved to bang its head to the front again.

As she touched the none existing wall, her locket rose. The button she hid flew into the wall that became visible and then disappeared straightaway.

The veil vanished, revealing a landscape of thick grass covering a field where a desolate manor with half of its roof missing stood in the middle.

Leviel's heart grew frigid as she took in its state. Half of the manor's gate's arch was on the ground, covered by moss and grass, far from its former grandeur.

A vision passed her eyes of a scythe, slicing through the very gate. She knew who the wielder was. *Thanatos Galen.* From what she gathered from her father, he removed the Kazis from authority and disbanded them. Kazi was the name for the ersatzes knights. This dilapidated mansion used to be their main headquarters.

She was sceptical about why they hid its existence here rather than leave it untouched.

Leviel wanted to know what happened here. Especially why did Galen slaughter them? Not just any Kazi, the Khycen knights. Too bad she's an ersatz, not a witch. Her powers aren't strong enough to envision the events before their ruin. No doubt her great granny could.

Leviel strolled to the near nonexistent cobbled pathway, buried by the pile of rotting leaves. Untrimmed evergreen trees flanked the sides. A gush of wind whirled earth debris around Leviel, and she buried her chin to her chest while rubbing the goosebumps on her arms.

When Leviel neared the manor, the bare botanical garden with its front missing drew her notice. It was on the left wing where soil blanketed the once marbled floor. Without warning, she heard a shriek, making her duck in reflex. She saw a fifteen-foot-tall greyish caramel owl swooping in her direction. Only for it to disappear before it could clamp its claws on her.

Leviel didn't know if it was a hallucination or real. It was lifelike and resembled the one that died in her arms years ago.

After regaining her composure, she marched into the manor only to freeze. The spacious foyer, decorated with a Persian red and gold rug, and the cabriole sofa parked at the sides of the staircase leading to the second-floor corridor were how it was four years ago. What's more disturbing, the hearth was burning as if expecting her visit. She saw the owl from earlier unmoving upstairs, perched at a pillar. Leviel teleported to it and touched its head.

It was still dead.

Melancholy sipped into Leviel's chest as she carried on, brushing the owl's back. She savoured the bitterness on her tongue before dropping her hand to her sides. But as she spun back, its chestnut-rimmed onyx eyes transfixed her, and a vision appeared.

Several eyespots on a butterfly's wings formed in her consciousness. It was identical to the one she painted when she was little. Uninterested, she whirled. A canvas with the same eyespots on the wall made her stop dead in her tracks. At the bottom right was her signature.

It can't be.

When Leviel said, 'little,' she meant a millennium ago.

Leviel felt lightheaded and staggered. Suddenly a force sucked her, pulling her below the foyer where now a beamed of light formed a pentagram. The button from her locket was at its centre, illuminating the energy that drew her like a magnet.

Perturbed by it, Leviel hurried, and she teleported herself outside the manor near a dried pond. If it weren't for the moonlight, darkness would have near covered the place.

Darkness? Leviel's heart pounded, making her chest burn. The sun was at its peak when she arrived at the student manor. *Why was it evening now?*

A shadowy figure looking out the window from upstairs appeared. It was of a young man holding a glass.

Scotch, Leviel thought while her eyes widened. *How did she know that?* Pain burst into her head, and she wanted nothing more than to rub her temples. To her horror, she couldn't move, for her hands were no longer hers. "Chrissake!" Her mother warned her this would happen if Leviel couldn't reign in her gift of sight—courtesy of Sirona's bloodline.

Leviel's visions pirouetted, and she now stood at the open windows while she watched the fireflies outside gathered in a sycamore tree. Her eyes followed their quick movements and glued on to the golden sparks falling in their wake. She honed on to a pair that remained beside the pool, weaving heart shapes on their path. Then a frog croaked as it hopped from one lotus leaf to another, startling the pair who spiralled off. But the heart shape remained for a few seconds and then died.

"If you were only a mere mortal, would you have given love a chance?" a little girl asked, sitting at the wooden pier while her legs dangled in the water.

Leviel shook her head in response. *Whose head am I in?*

"Rückgabe!"

Ice slid down her spine. She spoke in a man's voice. But before she could deduce the speaker, her vision spun, and she stared into the owl's eyes again.

Frightened, she ran outside, only to find the gates were out of her reach. She kept sliding back to the entrance as if on a treadmill. Still, Leviel continued as her legs grew heavier with each round until she lost consciousness.

Multiple golden moths swarmed Leviel's lifeless body. Some entered her forehead while the others pulled her to stand. Then, her locket opened, and the clock's hands spun fast counterclockwise and stopped. In an instant, a powerful force sucked her back to the manor while it restored itself to its former glory.

***

A lone golden moth burst out from Leviel's forehead and morphed into a figure in a royal blue fitted armour suit covered with a cream hood. Held in its arms was Capala, reduced to a normal-sized owl, belting. It escaped into the beaming light at the centre of the pentagram, dissolving into the air.

The lid of Leviel's locket fastened.

After a while, Leviel stirred and opened her eyes, feeling disoriented. "Bloody—where am I?" She touched her face and peeled off a brown leaf obstructing her view, meeting the hooded Kazi who hunched over her. The crest on the knight's mask was unmistakable. Judging by the shape of her chest, the knight was a woman.

Leviel felt the sogginess of the ground sip through her dress, and she shot off to her feet, crashing into the knight. The Kazi was akin to a projection—still and translucent.

A pain in her neck distracted her. Its source was her necklace. She opened it and saw the clock within was now turning clockwise, as it should. Leviel stretched her arms, and the button flew back to her hand. In an instant, the lid of the locket snapped closed, and the transparent figure disappeared.

"Leviel?" came a man's voice. Perhaps the announcer at the gatehouse.

It was only then that Leviel remembered she hadn't had the cherubs sort out her identity. *Can they still confirm her even if she is in a doppelt mode?* All first-year students must have a cherub verify their identity and divide them according to the House of the archangel they would serve. It was the final stage of their admittance to Galen.

Raphaelle, the archangel Leviel serves, has two houses under her jurisdiction—Tobit and Israfil.

Those under the House of Tobit are adept at healing ailments. Their graduates are celestial physicians now. The House of Israfil specialised in music to cure those who had gone mad. Then there are the cupids—the cherubs that create the mortal's happy meetings and mishaps of their fates. Both Tobit and Israfil house them.

Leviel possesses both Tobit's and Israfil's skills. But far from being a matchmaker. She'll leave it to the cherub to choose her House.

"Leviel? Is that you?" She saw Dove waving a hand on her face. Well, through her clone, that is. Dove prodded her dazed form.

Leviel eyed the ruined gate, then to the doors of the manor. In her current state, she didn't trust herself to teleport back to the uni gates where cherubs scrutinised and confirmed their identities. And not wanting for the pentagram to form again, she waved her finger, and a portal opened. She dashed in.

"Leviel!" came a man's voice again, making her speed up.

"Ow!"

A hulking body from her right collided with her, throwing her off several paces from her original path. Leviel reckoned this was akin to being hit by a truck at full speed as she howled. She knew right then she'd see several bruises on her arms tomorrow. And with the energy she expelled earlier from the manor, she doubts if she has enough to hasten her recovery.

"Sorry!" came a deep, hesitant voice.

Leviel found a knight in its silver and black chrome hauberk who lay unmoving, with his helmet covering his face. Its tiny slit wasn't enough for her to determine his condition from where she sat.

"Is he dead?" Leviel asked, shaking her head. "No. You just said sorry."

"My apologies," said the knight, who rolled to his sides before leaping back on his feet. He towered over Leviel and extended his hand to help her up.

Leviel ignored his hand and stood. But her eyes fixed on the shining insignia of half a tree and an eagle on his breastplate, matching his right knee shield.

"Leviel!" came again the announcer's voice.

She sensed her clone disappeared, making her scramble in haste to the portal's door. Only to step on the knight's sword and slip. "The hell is—" Leviel paused as an arm held her, broke her fall, and the opening slammed closed. "No!" Frustration marred her face, and she struggled to break his hold.

"Leviel?" the knight asked, dropping his hand.

She straightened herself, gave him a dagger look, and shoved him. "Why'd you have to run into me?" *Of all the most opportune moments.* Leviel ran to the closed exit and slid her hands, trying to find an invisible knob to open it.

"Sorry. You too caught me unaware," said the knight, who peered at the portal from where she had entered. "No one uses that entrance. At least, not anymore."

"Why isn't this opening?" Leviel asked as she kept thumping on the portal's door.

"It has a six to seven minutes interval."

"Brilliant! Just brilliant!"

The knight gave her a once over the exact moment she swung. "Are you a freshman?"

Leviel did the same, only to fix her gaze on his armour's crest. *My lord!* Her brows knitted, and she placed her hands on her hips. After a millennium, she saw a heavenly sentinel. She thought they'd gone extinct. Leviel was not counting the one from the in-between.

An actual sentinel of the heaven that answers orders from Michael or Raphaelle was standing there. She last crossed paths with them in her first life.

They specialised in stealth and reconnaissance and controlled the torches that lit up the diagram of the pleroma. It was the key that could open the three realms. And they can stand toe to toe with the gatekeepers.

"You're from the capital?" Leviel asked. The 'capital' was a joke between angels turned norm when referring to the heavenly realm.

The knight bobbed.

"Then shouldn't you have used the fastest route?" Leviel asked, gritting her teeth and rolling her eyes. She returned to tapping on the door again, but it didn't budge. "Did you hear me?"

"How'd you come about this portal?" Leviel's heart skipped, sensing danger as his voice turned soft.

The portal opened while she tried to think of an excuse and rushed out. Leviel realised too late that the opening was several feet from the ground. She braced for the impact when a force arrested her descent, holding her still suspended mid-air.

Fluffy clouds neared her while black wings unfolded on her back before her descent resumed. She gyrated as a mass of arrows shot at her. To Leviel's astonishment, she swirled as if she knew how to fly with wings. Another batch of arrows sailed to her. She had no time to ponder before her body moved, avoiding them. Then her eyes widened as she saw below a phalanx of archers in dark hooded cloaks readying their bows and arrows while aiming at her.

Why were the old sentinels mobilised? Against her? Well, was she even there?

Leviel wheeled again until she stood poised in the air. Two bright stars in the distance moved at an incredible speed. At the same time, a dark hovering clumping cloud a hundred feet above the ground formed a ball the size of a stadium.

"Keep your positions!" Leviel heard Absolute down below. The mortal was in Galen's army uniform, and she held a sword ablaze. "In a count of three." Absolute counted down with her fingers. "Fire!"

The angel's platoon leader, on Absolute's right, dropped his raised hands. The arrows went into the dark clouds.

It rained acid over them in return.

Undeterred, Absolute threw her flaming sword to the clouds. It broke, and the gargoyles came out and scattered atop the hill of corpses, including Dove's lifeless eyes and Sybil's limbless body.

Leviel jerked her gaze over the horizon, and without a thought, she flew in to stop the two colossal speeding stars heading toward each other. But before reaching it, her wings burned, and off the impact went.

When the ringing wave of fire settled, she saw the cherub from her dreams with a burgundy gem on its forehead. He held a glass globe where the mortal world still burned. Then, his midnight blue eyes locked with hers and crushed the globe.

The monster from her dreams came out, opened its gigantic mouth, and took a bite.

A dislocating pain on Leviel's shoulders woke her, and she found herself face down, still in mid-air. Below, the structure of Galen's towers and palaces appeared like miniatures. She glanced at her chest and discovered she was hanging by the sling of her side bag caught by the knight standing at the edge of the open portal.

"I supposed you're the source of your accidents," he smirked.

"Washing your hands, eh? It seems unfair, as my life is in your hands." Leviel glared at him before glancing down. A few students spotted her predicament.

"Should I just leave you here dangling until the admission is over?" he jested and raised his helmet's visor, revealing his teal-coloured eyes. "What do you say, Leviel?"

Her eyes dilated and turned sombre, locking with him. Without preamble, she yanked her bag and let herself fall. Large white wings came out behind the knight, but he froze as yellow-green mists covered Leviel, pulling her down until she stood straight on the ground.

He flew out like a beam, and the portal vanished.

Leviel turned to her saviour. *A witch*, she thought.

"Yes, a witch. By the by, you're welcome," said Sybil.

And she can read my mind.

"Of course. I'm an oracle. Why'd you fall from the sky? And what'd you see?"

"The view is excellent there." She would never admit to anyone that she was a seer.

"Without a doubt," said the voice which kept calling her earlier. Leviel first saw a pair of brogue shoes approaching her in haste. Then she gawked at the elderly, who stopped in front of her. "Now, Lady Leviel Khycen, do you still want to enter Galen?"

5

Mattaniah Evander

*O*n a wet Sunday morning, turmoil brews at the House of Adams. The Galen's student military huddled a few steps outside the main doors of the tower. They were in a standoff with the four-foot gargoyle standing at the vestibule cloaked in silver, barring them from getting in.

Meanwhile, by order of the student council, the soldiers placed a cordon to bar the humans from entering the premises. Lieutenant Illa Victor and his team carried it out, a not-so favourite by the humans. Regardless of him being one himself. Hence the trouble.

Of course, the students familiar with what it signified hurried to the nearest common library, where they took refuge—at least for now. The others who knew but remained don't care.

It may be the most exciting news for days to come. They wanted to be seen. So they ignored protocols and pretended to be fearless. No danger can stop their one minute of fame.

Not long after, shouts ensued. A riot may well be in order.

With testosterone flying about, it was only natural for the boys to test their temporary boldness against the student military. *Poor them,* Victor thought. They don't know whether to protect the mortals or feed them to the danger at the tower. Not that they know what happened. Except the mortals were in jeopardy if they remained near Adams. By the looks of things, whether a danger unto themselves or something else, Victor's money was in the former.

Half an hour later, four young men dressed in a dark coat with the Student Council's coat of arms materialised above them. They landed in the courtyard, exciting the clamouring crowd.

"What is going on, gov?"

"You can't leave us out in the cold!"

"GIVE US ANSWERS!"

Victor gestured to Delton Smythe—his sergeant who stepped out from the tower, oblivious to the two boys who took a gander and then craned closer to him.

"So?" Victor asked.

"More than a dozen students stayed over during the break. Three days ago, they had a party. Since then, none had seen them step out of the building," Smythe whispered. "When the steward returned from his holiday, Beastie," he pointed to the gargoyle, "Welcomed him."

"He must be in shock." Victor glanced at the creature, looking more amiable than its stone version atop the uni's main gates.

"Worst! He near had a heart attack," Smythe bobbed his head. "Poor man!"

"No. I meant it," said Victor as he tilted his head to the foyer before surveying the crowd. "At their outcry. An ungrateful bunch!" *They would have walked to their demise if it weren't for the gargoyle.*

"Tell me about it. I was here right away. The gargoyle only stared at me, but it appeared to claw me when I tried to climb the stairs. There must be something terrible up there."

"On that note, make sure they throw nothing at the gates. We can do nothing once it tore their heads off."

"Will do." Smythe spun and only now caught the two mortal boys. He whirled to Victor, "Or we can just leave them at their mercy."

Victor grinned at him as he radioed the information his sergeant shared. "They held the dog back. But negative on the mortals."

"Any word on the ministers?" Theodore asked over the radio. Like Victor, he was a lieutenant. But of the Galen army.

"Negative. There's no one here."

"EVANDER!" A mortal in the crowd waved at an approaching figure.

Victor followed his line of sight and only now saw Mattaniah Evander, the Vice Minister of the Student Council, who heeled their Chief Minister Haniel as he acknowledged the mortal with a nod, without breaking his stride.

They were the most approachable council members. But also the most formidable. So, the students stood compliant as they passed.

"Evander and the Chief, on their way. Over," said Victor on the radio.

"Got it."

The double doors slammed when the leaders went in, blocking the crowd's view. The furore resumed, and the uproar intensified.

***

Within the tower, at that moment, Lieutenant Theodore Rokeby came downstairs. He was conscious of the gargoyle's stares. He didn't know how to walk around it without stepping or bumping it.

"Rokeby," Mattaniah called his attention.

Theodore missed a step, and his face came close to the creature's nose. He squirmed but composed himself in time. It didn't seem proper to be skittish under their Vice Minister's watchful eyes. Rumour has it he defeated the mightiest General of the immortals a month ago. It would be nice if he could get inside his regiment.

"The smell of a rotten corpse dominated the floor above, but not a single body is in sight." Despite Theodore's pretence, he ascended two steps to distance himself from Beastie.

"Odd." Mattaniah jammed his hand in his pocket while gesturing for the other four council members to go upstairs. "Haniel, what do you think?"

"It's one of ours," said their Chief, staying near the windows, observing the happenings.

Mattaniah examined the gargoyle, and with no fear, he spread its bat-like wings. "He doesn't seem to sustain any injuries."

"Mayhap it summoned it."

Mattaniah waved his hands behind his back, and the beast disappeared while he glared at Haniel's back.

Serves him right, Theodore thought. Their Chief appeared unconcerned. Haniel then glimpsed at Theodore, making him set his sights back on Mattaniah. He forgot Haniel was an angel and could read his thoughts.

"A monster on the loose doesn't sit well with me." Mattaniah rounded the hall.

There's a monster out there? Within Galen University? It must not be a simple one as it got past Beastie. Or his pals at the gates, Theodore's mind rioted, forgetting to mask his terror.

Mattaniah waved his hand once more, and the gargoyle materialised.

Surprised, Theodore stumbled off the steps, but he felt a hand on his back, steadying him before reaching the landing. When he peered behind, he saw Beastie's dark paw on his back. He couldn't help but swallow a nonexistent bolus as he grasped the handrail.

"Thank you," said Theodore to the beast, who spread one of its wings as a reply.

"How certain are we that the cherubs have not admitted a hybrid?" Mattaniah carried on.

"It's out of the question. Three cadres were there." Haniel eyed Mattaniah.

"Is there a chance one of them was complacent? There's three of them, after all."

Haniel's jaw dropped, and his eyes fluttered. "Perfunctory has never been part of our dictionary. I feel insulted, by the way. And I'm sure you know we're not prone to human errors—especially an archangel."

"But everyone still makes mistakes," said Mattaniah, meeting Haniel's dark face. He raised both hands, giving up. "I know. Not the time. Not the place. But that statement wasn't for you." He paused and peered upstairs. So did Theodore. No one was paying attention to their talk except for the soldier. "If not an error. Then it was deliberate."

I didn't just hear that! I'm still here. Theodore summoned all ounces of his will and contrived to appear as a statue. *Hear no evil. See no evil.*

Haniel now appeared as if he wanted to smack his deputy's head. But a thought stopped him. *Perhaps they were heedless of its presence—by design.* However, it won't bode well to admit the chaotic politics in the capital. Before he could retort, a legionary angel appeared.

Its nearness was too bright for Mattaniah's comfort, who marched to the windows, gazed out, and remained fixated. He spotted a person looking straight at him, who towered over the others and swayed along with the push and tugged from the crowd.

"It's code red. The Grigoris have breached our portals."

The Legionary bobbed to Haniel.

"W-wait! What?" Haniel asked, whose eyes glowed akin to teal sapphires. But the warrior angel vanished before he could move to stop him.

Mattaniah swung and found Haniel in shock.

"Chief!"

"What—alright! I'll leave this case to your hands." Haniel stretched his arm toward Beastie. "I give you leave to explore your theories." Without another word, he vanished along with the gargoyle.

"Excellent!" Mattaniah stared at the spot where the gargoyle sat earlier. A pair of tiny black squares marred the smooth floor. He stooped to touch it and found a dark powdery residue. "Charcoal."

Fire? Theodore wondered.

"Why is she here once again?" Mattaniah muttered and cast his eyes back to the man he observed outside.

The young man's grey-teal-coloured eyes turned into onyx as if he heard his thoughts, bobbed his head and then disappeared.

"It appears my theory was far off from the truth."

What theory? Theodore wanted to ask.

A lightning bolt struck Mattaniah without warning, who glowed, covered in blue light. He winked at Theodore before his form disintegrated.

"But weren't you a mortal?" Theodore asked, glancing at the ceiling.

A clap of thunder was his answer.

6

Love Dust

*T*hat afternoon, Leviel heaved as she ran through a walkway of thick beech trees, whose leaf-bearing branches formed an arch canopy. A smell of fresh air with a hint of mint besieged her nostrils as she neared its end. Rooted eucalyptus trees flanked the sides with near-empty benches parked between the tree's trunk.

Leviel felt a sudden creeping pain in the pit of her stomach. Yesterday, during her run, both new and older students occupied most of the benches. She assumed most would come out to play today. Ignoring its oddity, she ran down the steps leading to a hanging tree bridge and noticed its sudden wobbling. She teleported to the centre of the bridge and saw none in sight.

A punch came up to her face. With quick reflex, she ducked, then blocked a kick on her right side, meeting a pair of bird claws. She teleported away, but not before it scratched her. The wounds disappeared in a blink. Two angels in a button-downed suit materialised while she felt a searing pain on her left arm, where her armband should have been.

The angel behind her hit her and found his hands covered in a greenish flame. It crept to his shoulders. On instinct, he pressed two fingers on it, cutting his burning arm. A dozen white doves burst out from the severed part and morphed to form a new arm.

Gatekeepers?

Too bad the red and black strings used to wrap around Leviel's arms from her previous life were missing. It was a good choice of weapons against Gabrielle's angels.

Leviel jumped out of the way when the other stretched his arms to grab her neck. Although she avoided it, she hit her head at a redwood tree supporting the bridge.

"I do not quarrel with you. Why are you—"

A throbbing pain afflicted her head, rendering her mute, and the scenes from the ruined manor assaulted her.

Frosty hands touched her forehead, and the pain faded. Leviel gazed at her saviour. It was the cream-cloaked Kazi. A sword appeared in her hand and stabbed the gatekeeper on her left. Then, at lightning speed, she slashed the other.

As dark clouds swirled above, the gatekeepers dissolved into doves, doubling by the second while the temperature dropped to wintry. A sparkling blue light appeared at the sides, enshrouding the birds, and they vaporised into snowflakes. The Kazi was nowhere on site. She batted her eyes. Everything was back to normal, like it had never happened.

A young man in a Student Council coat appeared in place of the doves. Embroidered letters above the crest read Mattaniah Evanders. "Go!" His cold sapphire eyes fixed on her, sucking her thoughts in, and her visions swirled.

Leviel found herself running to a small pathway in the middle of a lime chartreuse-coloured meadow while dusk settled over the welkin. Petals of the same shade glided in the wind while a stinky smell assailed her.

Her eyes widened.

It was the same field she had appeared in after Briana died. And before her reincarnation into this lifetime. *Was this a reminder?*

Leviel can't perceive if the encounter from the bridge was only a vision. Or, worst, a hallucination. She had too many dreams to sort. The next second, she recalled the purpose of her run. Leviel wanted to reach the courtyard of the old sentinel's holding before the light disappeared. With gatekeepers on her heels, she might as well return.

Feeling tired, she stopped, took three sips of water, and wiped the sweats on her face. Leviel scanned the landscape again. The place looked deserted. Leviel knew several took this route for an early evening run.

Not again! Mayhap everyone turned in earlier than yestereve? While she shook off the dread, two dark figures swirled past her. An icy sweat slid down her spine.

One figure with wings dressed in a roman legionary armour lunged his sizzling lance at an aquamarine-eyed being she knew well not to be trifled with. The latter's dark suit was new to her. She was only familiar with either his fiery form or his reaper's robes.

He tilted to the right as his wings disappeared, deflecting the onslaught. The warrior's lance hit the ground while a force kept it there.

"What was that for?" he asked as he adjusted his necktie.

The warrior didn't answer at once. He was exerting much force to pull his lance back. Then the hold vanished, making him stumble. He could only glare at the other being as he righted himself. "You've brought some company, your highness."

A portal opened above, and a dozen dark smoky figures stepped out. They turned into a gargoyle with a near ten-foot-long wingspan blaring fire. Three legionary warriors locked closed to their wings.

Leviel stood struck as she watched a mix of white and black wings rioting above and below as the warriors tried to suppress the gargoyles. Her knees quivered, praying none would notice her.

"You mistook me for your liege. GET ON WITH IT."

The divine creature snickered while removing his necktie. He then raised his blazing hands. Before the warrior at the side could raise his lance to join his angels, an electric bluish light materialised between them and the gargoyle. It morphed into a man in a shirtless brown-coloured suit.

Leviel couldn't help but compare his blues with Evander's, espying a half-burned oren tattoo on his neck. Then her eyes landed on his face, making her blink. She rubbed her eyes to be sure.

What a beautiful specimen, Leviel thought so.

A chuckle came behind her. She spun, but none was there.

"Well, Midael, take care of it," said the seraph, addressing the handsome newcomer, now in his armour.

Midael? Leviel fixed her gaze on the warrior's half-crest plume on his helmet at the mention of his name. The name sounded familiar.

A shield engulfed the fight with the wave of the fiery being's hands. It sealed the battle from outsiders.

"Metro, what are you doing here?" Midael asked the warrior who attacked his Highness.

Metro? Michael's current right hand?

Leviel blinked.

"I was here the whole time you were kissing—"

Metro's powers died as if someone sucked them from his body.

"Close the portal. RIGHT NOW!" said Midael. A sword of scintillating blue flames appeared in his hand.

"I'm trying my utmost to do just that!"

The gargoyles charged at the shield itself, making Leviel take several steps back. She didn't know whether to stay or run. Either way, it would distract the gargoyles and attack her instead. Meanwhile, a monstrous-sized, dark hooded figure with wings akin to the gargoyle's peered at the portal. It didn't take long before the warrior's curses grew as the gargoyles increased their size.

Midael's twenty-foot-long ivory wings spread wide while he aimed his sword at the portal. The energy on the blade now gained momentum. It evolved akin to a hundred whips sailing around to fight off the creature, whose enormous shadow shrouded the canola field as it descended.

Leviel tried to discern what it was when a thunderous rumble made her hide behind a shrub.

"Shit, no!"

The blade on Midael's sword died out, and the monstrous being passed them in a swift. It hurled everything out of its way, including Leviel, who near hit a tree.

She tried to examine her injuries. But the thick soot hindered her. Even if she could, it wasn't their average fog under normal conditions.

"Hold them off," said Midael, who flew after it.

"Was that him?"

"For the love of—"

"Bloody HELL!"

"Why'd you let him pass?"

As the warriors scrambled to hold the gargoyles off, a splash of light radiated away from the shield, throwing her several paces. Nearby trees split, uprooting shrubs at the sides. Grass needles flew in all directions.

A few seconds, several detonations succeeded but were benign compared to the first blast.

"Good, some help!" Leviel heard laughter within the centre of the explosion and cheers.

While sprawled, Leviel released a long breath, only discovering now she was holding it in. The fog cleared, and Leviel noticed the scrapes she sustained disappeared. She leaned on her elbows and sat upright, only to find a pair of derby beside her.

Its owner stood looming over her while his aquamarine eyes locked on hers.

"I-I d-didn't s-see anything," Leviel knelt.

He hunched to cover her eyes. "Then how'd you know that would be my question?"

"Wai—" Leviel stretched her arms in front, wanting him to step back. But he was like the redwood tree, sturdy and rooted.

"Your Highness. I shall take care of the young ersatz," came a deep voice, who smirked, making Leviel pause. She fisted while the hand on her face fell.

The sentinel she met at the portal stood behind without a helmet, revealing his ivory-coloured military-cut hair and a face that matched Midael's beauty.

He was there all the time, eh? Leviel's brows knitted as she stared at his smooth porcelain cheeks. Something was missing, Leviel thought, but could not discern it.

"Very well," said his Highness while a fiery light cloaked his body, and he vanished.

The sentinel stepped closer to her, "It seems we're not to meet under fortunate circumstances."

Too shaken from meeting Samael—the heavenly commander, Leviel sat on her legs. The knight's arm stretched out to support her.

I shall take care of the young ersatz, still echoed in Leviel's mind, making her shove his arms. But the sentinel didn't budge.

Sparks of red light appeared at the sides, morphing to Thomas—head of Tobit and Israfil.

Good, he's here. However, it seemed a tad too late for her appointment as a heartbreaker. She has known him since she was little. To be precise, Thomas is her godfather, a pure angel although he looks younger than her, and always her bearer of bad news on her fifteen birthdays. Well, until this time.

The angels bobbed at each other. The next instant, Leviel was in Thomas's arms while the sentinel put on his helmet. "I leave her to your care." Leviel wanted to struggle, but her vision blurred, and she lost consciousness.

***

When she arose from fainting, her arm shielded her eyes from the bright light. She had an IV needle in her hand. Pink curtains flanked the bed she laid on, while no drapery covered the front floor-to-ceiling window. The space was only enough for her to spread her arms.

Sensing someone neared, she turned to her right, where the curtains slid to the sides, revealing Thomas. "Excellent, you're awake." He strode and sat at the foot of the bed.

Leviel's aches all over dissipated. She knew it was courtesy of the angel. However, the pain in the back of her head remained. It jolted her memory, displaying the scenes from the meadow akin to a movie in her mind. "How did I—"

"Although Haniel asked me to take care of you, I only follow her grace's order. Until the Marshall decides your fate or a request from the left-hand commander arrives, you can keep your memory now," said Thomas, interrupting her in his no-nonsense voice. "You know what you have to do."

Pretend nothing happened, said Leviel via telepathy.

Indeed, Thomas bobbed while Leviel glared.

53

She dropped her gaze and sat up. A thought crossed her mind. "I've been meaning to rid my mind of this question. Am I still a heartbreaker?"

The curtains swayed open, baring rows of hospital beds, saving Thomas from replying. But none appeared in between the gap. Leviel looked down and found two cherubs. One with burgundy hair and bright blue eyes and the other with thick golden hair whose cute wings had difficulty taking his chubby body off the ground. Both had bow and arrow holders slung over their shoulders.

"When do we go home?" the burgundy-haired cherub asked with mirth dancing in his eyes.

"Leviel here had recovered. We can leave at any moment, although she's still weak," said Thomas, carrying the little one. He turned to her. "Do return this to Haniel." He pointed to the cape covering her before turning to the cherub in his arms. "Where's Coviel?"

"I'll help you heal," came a cute voice of a young auburn-haired cherub who climbed onto her bed.

Coviel, she presumed. Leviel must still be on the mend, as her hearing and sight senses weren't keen enough to catch him. Coviel swooped above her, sprinkling red-golden dust all over her.

"Stop!" Thomas reached out to catch him, but hit the wall instead.

"Idiot! It won't heal her," said another cherub in a monk's robe who flew in from the open curtains. Contrary to his words, he sailed to Leviel's head, sprinkling thicker dust on her arms. "It's love's dust, not a panacea."

"A what?" Leviel's eyes widened, then knitted her brows. She covered her exposed arms with the cloak.

"He's joking," said Thomas, letting go of the cherub in his arms. Then pulled the nursling in a monk's robe. He covered the cherub's mouth before it could protest. The other two cherubs followed Coviel.

"But Raphaelle said it can help," said Coviel, carrying on with showering dust.

It alarmed Leviel more, and she waved her arms to shoo them, but it only made them hover more.

"He's right on that matter. It'll speed up your recovery," said Thomas, trying not to laugh, taking the two cherubs far from her reach.

Leviel's instinct tells her Thomas wasn't telling her the whole truth. "What cherubs are these?" pointing to them despite knowing fully what the bows and arrows signify. The little ones had the gall to grin at her.

"They're the real deal," said Thomas with a straight face.

"The ones that turned to real angels when they grew up?"

The little ones bobbed their heads again.

Thomas swallowed as he averted his eyes and said, "Purebreds—raised by her grace personally."

"CUPIDS!" Leviel leapt off the bed as she shrieked. The cherubs dove and hid behind Thomas. "Why did you let them near me?" She scrubbed the sparkling powders only to find them stuck to her hands.

"No—no!" Thomas reached out to stop her. "Don't think about a man."

"Who's Haniel, by the way?" Leviel asked as Thomas' words fell.

Both of them paused.

"Too bloody late for that now," Thomas recovered first and backed away. "To answer your question, Haniel is the sentinel from the meadow." He pulled the cherubs out, who obeyed and stayed behind the curtain. Then faced her. "Go back after you finish the IV bag and be careful on your way. A monster is on the loose. I heard it killed more than a dozen mortals Friday night. To my dismay, the SC and the military students failed to apprehend it. Not that I placed any faith in them. I reckoned the army will be here."

"Oh," said Leviel. It came out without a thought.

"And when I mean 'army,' it's Thanatos's soldiers."

Is it such a coincidence that she's been dreaming of a monster? Leviel's mind was in a riot.

Heedless of her thoughts, Thomas threw a scroll at her. She caught it using her left hand. "Her grace might call on you soon."

He gazed at her for a minute and believed he had diverted her attention elsewhere other than the love dust. So he tugged the curtains together and left her.

After finishing the fluid bag, Leviel pulled the needle and left the infirmary of Tobit. Leviel glanced at the white cloak on her arms and then opened the scroll. It was the same as the ones she always received on her fifteenth birthday. Except now, they did not assign her to Absolute Trench or Talitha. The letter written in gold ink had only one line:

Michael-Shiphrael-Lucifer

Leviel rolled it back and felt a blast of icy draft blanketing her body as she exited the gates. She donned the cloak at once. She discovered that only a part of her arms were visible to her. The guards roving at the main entrance of the manor village didn't notice as she passed while the hounds remained asleep. It was no wonder she overlooked Haniel after hearing him chuckle.

As she arrived at the small gate of her lodgings, she saw the manor's windows still had their lights on. And well-lit despite the hour, judging by the visible dark blue skies. As she drew closer, a chink came from an oak tree.

A witch's chime! Why would Mrs Z place one at the manor?

Minutes went by, but the woman-er-witch didn't appear.

"Adh." Silent. Leviel's eyes gleamed in the darkness. The jingling ceased. Like a thief, she sneaked into their manor using the near woody ivy vines, careful not to step on the lavender-coloured floral creepers at the foot. When she reached her room on the second floor, daylight had already crept in. She took a quick bath and readied for her class. It was one advantage as an ersatz—they never needed much sleep.

"Ahh!" came a scream.

Leviel jumped and dropped the bottle of lemon-scented oil. She teleported to the source, Absolute-er-Talitha's bedroom. In the middle of a queen-size bed, Talitha was writhing while mumbling, locked in her dream. She marched to the bed, but a bump from behind pushed her.

"OW!" Leviel ended up sprawled.

"Sorry!" said Sybil in her nightgown.

"What are you doing here?"

"I could say the same for you," said Sybil, gritting her teeth.

Leviel looked heavenward, stood, and walked to Talitha's bed.

An electric field repelled her.

Sybil noticed it too and waved her hand. A greenish, transparent shield came up, blanketing Talitha.

"It's enchanted," said Sybil.

"I can see that!"

Leviel shut her eyes and pressed two fingers on her forehead. Golden butterflies came out of her head, soared past the veil, straight into Talitha's forehead. A feather-like mole appeared in between her brows. It ignited.

The surrounding barrier thinned.

Leviel teleported through the shield and reached for Sybil. "Wa—Wait!" Sybil braced for the pain, but none came. "Oh! That's interesting." Her brows furrowed. She touched the shield that felt like concrete. "Someone did a great job of locking her in her dreams."

"A WITCH!" Leviel gave Sybil an icy stare.

"Why are you always like that? As if you aren't one of us."

"Am I? My mother's an ersatz. And I'm Camdiel's daughter. AND NO. No, no. Don't divert the topic. The barrier was a witch's doing."

"You can't know for certain," Sybil shook her head in denial. "Still, your blood has half of our kind. And for sure, inherited a sizeable chunk of your powers from Sirona."

"Aluel was born an ersatz."

"There's no point in winning with you. Do you also believe what the others say? That it was your mother's blood that brought the Kazi's downfall?" Sybil knew she was treading on hot water, bringing it up. But she has to say her point. "The angels wanted your unique abilities until you became useless to them. It's why they got rid of your line."

"If your kind is so innocent, why is a witch preying on Talitha?"

At least it's not me.

Leviel smirked as she heard Sybil's thoughts. *You're the only witch in the manor.*

It wasn't Mrs Z, for sure. She was not strong enough for Shiphrael.

Before Sybil could rebuff her, Leviel vanished and was behind her in a flash. She felt a tap on her shoulders. "No time to argue with you, witch." Leviel spun Sybil, who now stood frozen.

Remove your hold!

Leviel carried on examining the witch's mind. Disappointed, she let go and removed her power's hold. She was indeed telling the truth. Sybil pushed her in return, but Leviel stepped to the side, making her flail in the air and trip. Leviel steadied her, halting her fall. Sybil's lashes batted, stunned by her quick reflex.

Unaware of Sybil's regard, Leviel whirled just in time to see the slight movement on the bed.

"She's awake."

"Splendid!" Sybil reached to touch Talitha's head, but Leviel held her arm halfway.

"Don't touch her. I can't allow you to harvest her memories."

What are you implying? I only want to calm her, said Sybil, and pulled her arm back.

She looks calm to me. Too quiet for comfort. Leviel crossed her arms on her chest.

Whatever! Sybil turned to Talitha and asked, "Bad dreams?"

Talitha winced and sat upright while Leviel gave Sybil a hard stare.

Why'd you have to state the obvious?

"Girls! Breakfast is ready," came Mrs Z's voice from downstairs.

Leviel and Sybil scrambled out and left Talitha's room.

"I'll tell granny Sisi about this," Sybil warned her in the hallway.

"As if I fear, Sirona," she said, giving her a hither look.

Sybil gawked and then walked away while Leviel returned to her room.

Upon entering her chambers, the butterflies from earlier sailed back inside Leviel's forehead, and she collapsed.

Darkness greeted her.

A few seconds later, Talitha's glowing figure popped and faded into an enormous inky cloud.

It morphed into a monstrous serpent with burgundy eyes glowing, as was the claret-coloured gem on its forehead.

"Oh, look at that! Like the others, you're taken aback by how fast my outer body is dwindling by the day. I believed even 'the dark prince' has discerned my predicament," a woman's voice came. "You said you've killed her!"

"Mistress, she indeed died."

"Find that child, the one with Shiphrael's heart. Make sure that she doesn't lose it."

"Yes, Mistress."

The beast's eyes became sombre and clawed the walls while a blazing fire grew thicker, cloaking everything in sight before it roared.

Its voice made Leviel quiver. She didn't just hear the dark prince?

"Ahh!" Talitha screamed, and the scene changed to a dark room before a brilliant light came. The most beautiful girl she had ever seen in her life floated, surrounded by puffy white clouds. Her raven hair sailed while her porcelain skin shone.

"Wake up!"

"You!" the dark prince called. "Stop! Don't go!" The serpent's image faded.

Shiphrael appeared poised above a dark pool with her fiery purple eyes. Flashes of turbulent lightning veiled her.

"You are thirsting for the truth, heartbreaker," said Shiphrael, who revealed to her the gold and red arrow lodged in her chest. "I'll let you cut the real chord this time."

7

Favour

An hour later, Leviel followed Talitha to the campus grounds for their first day of classes. She has not a single clue how she could achieve her mission. Everything's complicated. *Oh, life. It always is.* Leviel blew air into her mouth until her cheeks puffed. She's regretting going there. Maybe getting married wasn't such a bad idea. Talitha is still in her mortal form. *How would she determine which was Talitha's and which was Shiphrael's?*

"Hey!" called out Tirzah, running behind them, all dolled up in another tailored dress. She ran after them, tapped Leviel's back, and when she shrugged, Tirzah linked her arm to hers and the other to Talitha. Leviel tried hard to remove the mortal's arm, but it felt too tight. To her surprise, it won't budge.

"Well, fancy that." Leviel gritted her teeth.

"I'm so glad I caught up with you. Oh, there's Faber. Did you know he can morph into a giant boar—"

Tirzah chattered away as they walked side by side. She was not the least worried that her voice echoed down the road. Or that they don't know half of whom she spoke of.

Shall we throw her into the pond? Leviel suggested via telepathy as they near a footbridge.

Good idea. But we can't bully the mortals. It's written in the handbook.

Talitha grinned at Leviel, appearing undisturbed by the quacking.

Leviel reckoned they could only thank fate that they'd met Tirzah near the campus's gate and not at the manor.

A few minutes later, they arrived at the keep with a golden plaque framed with the word 'College of Celestial Arts.' The student military soldiers stood at the entrance and eyed them as they stepped in.

Leviel felt the slight tightening of Tirzah's arm, making her raise a brow. She gave her a side glance. "Interesting." But her gazes did not bother the mortal.

Inside the foyer, the glass pyramid ceiling akin to the Louvre drew her the most as otter clouds hovered outside, which wasn't present if you were outdoors. They passed the vast, long bleak gallery, flanked by arch windows and long tables with several lamps lit—though not enough to subdue the gloom.

Their lecture hall was an open space with a milky way galaxy projected on the ceiling and seats arranged in rows of circles akin to an amphitheatre. Given the size of the hall, the crowd was unexpected. Only a handful of seats were available for them. *With still another fifteen minutes to go? He must be some celebrity.*

Leviel observed the niches of students of different creatures lingering along the pathway and the back. The three took the centre seats four rows from the front.

Tirzah wanted to arrange their seating. "Oh, Leviel, the seat on my right—"

Leviel strode past the seat and took the third chair from it. "I think this chair most suited me," she said before Tirzah's last words could fall. She grinned as she laid her memo pad and pen on the table. Talitha didn't care about Tirzah's preference and took a bite of her sandwich, settling on the chair between them.

Tirzah sulked and turned to the group of girls at their front. Soon Tirzah's babbling dominated their conversation.

"A fallen soldier, they say, would be our lecturer," said Wilhelmina, a gaunt-looking mortal in a yellow sleeveless blouse and beige pleated skirt.

"A fallen angel?" Leviel asked, revealing she was eavesdropping. Not that it was a big deal. She was not the only one who could hear or read other beings' thoughts. "A Grigori?"

"Not the sort they kick out of grace." Wilhelmina peered at her, then faced the others. "Limited print copies. Only for the angels." She showed them a flyer with a picture of their lecturer. The girls squealed. "With that face, I wouldn't wonder. Looked at Luci-er-the dark Prince."

"Shh!" Tirzah didn't want them to mention the damned. So, she veered the topic to their speaker. Not long, she spun to Leviel and Talitha. "They say he looks very handsome."

Talitha, who, like Leviel, didn't hide her listening in, bobbed.

Leviel shrugged. She lost interest in their lecturer when the mortals ignored her. Instead, she was busy trying to read Talitha's thoughts and hid her smile. The word handsome piqued Talitha's interest, and she had listened since then.

"Ladies and gentlemen, please take your seats as we are about to start your class," came a female voice over the speaker. The small, scattered groups took their seats and listened in. Leviel felt crowded, and a throbbing pain began in her right temple. "Please welcome, Professor Eduard Galen."

She fixed her eyes on the entrance and froze.

My foot! Fallen angel?

Now she understood why she felt suffocated. It was the legionary from the meadow, Midael. His three-piece suit covered half of his oren, but its effect on her was the same as yestereve. She seldom gave a compliment. The crowd of students could not look away from him and held their breath. Even the witches and immortals alike were star-struck as the mortals.

They seem to be oblivious to what he is. Not caring would be the apt description. Given that the introduction prior didn't omit that he was a heavenly soldier, which Leviel knew well—he still is, despite rumours. But for sure, he's a master of disguise, she concluded. A legionary cannot hide his oren. It was why they knew who was Michael's soldier—until he. She would have mistaken him for a mortal without his tattoo.

Without warning, Leviel felt her mind being torn apart. Sweats beaded on her forehead, and the colour drained from her face as she fought the prober. But it was too powerful. Leviel could only watch her hands gripping the table while she mentally tried to subdue it.

In the next second, the tattoo on her arm opened. She covered it before anyone could see, regretting too late for removing her armband. Overwhelmed by her unknown enemy, her mother's blood tries to overcome it, and the hint of blue in her eyes covered its silverness, and they gleamed. She scanned the students.

"Are you all right?" Tirzah asked.

Leviel only knitted her brows further as she gazed to the front. Her blues locked with Eduard's purple ones.

It's him. Why?

In a blink, Eduard appeared beside her on her left while seeing him still standing at the centre, eyeing Talitha.

The image of the hall disappeared. A thick mist-covered lake came into her view while she stood atop the end of a wooden boat and Professor Galen at the opposite.

"Greetings, heartbreaker. What do you know of the monster?"

Leviel batted her eyes as she digested what had happened.

"I give you my word I shan't harm you."

Leviel shrugged, then rolled her eyes, letting him know the place wasn't welcoming.

Eduard chuckled, and they teleported to the middle of a road where a pile of scattered amber leaves surrounded a table flanked by two chairs. Above them, boughs of ginkgo trees spread, forming a tunnel. The rancid smell wasn't ideal but better than a frigid lake. He pulled a chair before gesturing for her to sit down.

Trapped in Eduard's dominion, there wasn't much room to object. Leviel felt saddened at the thin strings wrapped around her arms. Had it been before, then she could wipe an entire army. Since she only received her duties now, it can't help her. The strings aren't enough to stop a low-grade gatekeeper. Let alone Gabrielle's nemesis.

Before the fall, a nursling angel obscured behind the limelight of heaven's most beautiful angels, Lucifer and Shiphrael, duelled with Gabrielle.

By accident, they discovered his manipulation skills were on par with the archangel.

Being only a cherub then, the nursling near lost his life. Not only that, the fight stopped him from carrying on as a gatekeeper, and he has since become one of Michael's mightiest soldiers.

As the heir to the Khycen clan, Leviel quite knew the ranks in Michael's army. Midael's helmet had half a crest yesterday, which meant she was dealing with Michael's former right hand in command.

A smell of mint mixed with sandalwood disturbed her preoccupation before a white teacup on a saucer appeared. The server was laying them before her. When she caught his eyes, she almost leapt to her feet. It was Dr Errapel of Zywei Mole & Gen Research Lab. After pouring tea into Eduard's cup, he bowed and left.

"Your butler?" Leviel asked, trying to include humour to the impasse.

Eduard nodded before taking a sip of his tea. "I prefer coffee. But since I do not know how you wanted your coffee, it's tea for now. It's how—"

"I met the monster the day your butler appeared on a television debate. It was with Terra Obi regarding GMOs. I've been dreaming about him for years." Leviel cut to the chase. Eduard eyed her as if waiting for her to elaborate. "It has silver-teal eyes, but when it transforms into a mortal's figure, it changes to onyx." Leviel released a long breath. "It has the silverness of my eyes. At least most of the time."

"And each time does he kill?"

Leviel nodded.

"A child always appears afterwards. But I could not determine its sex, as it always changes within that dream or the next."

"What do you think of the killings?"

"Justified and unfair," said Leviel, peering at him over the teacups' rim.

She waited for Eduard to disagree with her and continued when he didn't. "It does not differentiate the innocent from the guilty. Worst, it reminded us we're all dispensable."

Eduard bobbed, removed his necktie and unbuttoned his shirt, exposing his neck with the oren tattoo. "Have you ever seen a similar tattoo to this engraved on a wooden chest?"

"No," said Leviel outright.

Eduard grinned.

Without warning, the scene changed, this time into a darkened forest with dead oak trees around her. "You lied," came a voice. When Leviel spun, a dead oak tree morphed into a giant, hooded black figure with a scythe. The figure's pointing finger waved at her. The visions of Talitha's endless deaths passed. Still, the angel of death kept waving his finger at Leviel, denying her life's continuity each time.

One cannot harm another being without harming oneself, a soft voice spoke in her mind. Then Death morphed into a dark-silver chromed legionary shrouded in darkness. Only his gleaming sapphire eyes stared her down. Then the scene changed into a river flanked by well-lit buildings while a canopy of peach blossoms hung above. Now the table sat in the middle of the river.

She and Eduard sat facing each other. He had his necktie and shirt back.

"We somehow share an affinity. I, too, suffered because of the commander's choices. So I shan't probe you further about the monster," said Eduard, gesturing at her tea. "Drink before it gets cold."

"Thank you." Leviel took a sip and drank in comfort.

"I need a favour, though." Eduard's voice was too soft. If it weren't for her keen sense of hearing, she might not hear it. Still, the word 'favour' made her choke on her drink. She bobbed her head to allow him to continue. "Can you see a red chord on me?"

With one brow raised, Leviel stared at Eduard's chest, then shook her head.

His face glowed in an instant. "What a relief!"

"I see a cupid's arrow lodged in your chest." Leviel raised her hand. "But its chord isn't visible to me. Unless I find your pair."

"Find it and break it for me," he said in an icy tone. His face darkened.

What is it with these angels asking her to break their love life? His request wasn't rare. Other beings who find love as weakness had approached her. As if it wasn't an insult to Raphaelle's department. *Mayhap Eduard's one of them.* Except for Shiphrael. Her case is rare. Perhaps Leviel's existence was for hers alone. The others are just a result.

"Midael, is it?" Leviel asked, giving him a forced smile.

"Oh, where are my manners? Toutes mes excuses," Eduard stood. "I'm Midael, formerly Commander of the Legionary. I have many names living with the mortals. But I am Professor Eduard Galen at the moment." He bobbed his head, then stretched his hand for a handshake.

"Ich bin erfreut Sie kennenzulernen. Under different circumstances." She shook his hands and bobbed. "Leviel Khycen."

"Pareil ici." Eduard went to his seat and poured himself another cup of tea. Leviel placed her cup back on its saucer and gave the young commander a helpless look. "I shall help you. In return, I need a favour."

Eduard smirked, "All right."

"Help me stop Shiphrael."

A powerful force pulled Leviel from Eduard's mental domain out of the blue. Her consciousness spun, and she was sitting in the lecture hall facing him. "I hope this lecture will improve your day immensely." Then he switched on his laptop, and a PowerPoint slide appeared on the whiteboard with the heading, 'the fall.'

Professor Sir, said Leviel, trying to call his attention.

Hang on.

Eduard began with an overview of the creation of angels. And on he went on.

Multi-tasking via telepathy wasn't a skill of an ersatz. Leviel might be back in reality, but the painful probing on her head doubled. She believed two forces were playing tug of war. One was opening her mind while the other was shutting the lid. The latter being the more painful.

Another minute passed before the forces on her head disappeared. It was like being thrown from the top of Everest. Leviel let the ease wash over her and gradually regained her bearings. She glanced around and caught the eyes of a bronze-skinned student in a red turban. He was sitting beside Lady Aliya Shuruppak. The man bobbed at her. A minute later, he averted his eyes from her.

"Never mind her," said Eduard, flicking his fingers. All eyes were on him now. "She must have heard the facts more times than anyone."

Laughter broke out again.

Leviel glanced to her right and found Talitha dozing. *It must be nice to sleep without a care.* Envious of her, Leviel stretched her arms to get comfortable in her seat.

I gave her leave to sleep. You, I have not.

Given Midael's rank and the Kazi's order, Leviel had no choice but to sit straight.

Oui, Commandant.

8
Tears in Heaven

Perhaps to add enthusiasm to those who find it too simple, their next class, Celestial Arts, tasked them to identify statues of divine beings inside a maze.

Still, Leviel found it wasn't as interesting as learning history through a legionary's eyes.

Believing her disinterest as apprehension, Dove lent her a book. It is like a cheat sheet of the figures in the maze. However, it was unnecessary. Leviel was older than Galen, the province itself. She was all familiar with them.

Leviel observed that there were several entrances to the maze. When their instructor signalled for them to begin, she went through the opened small gate, flanked by white columns where tiny female angels in a dress stood atop. Upon entering, a vast manicured lawn greeted her. A knee-high length hedge divided it to form a road in the middle. It brought her to a descending stair leading to one statue on the list.

She fixed her camera and took a photo of the figure. With her abilities, it was superfluous. But the school requires they adjust to the mortal's condition, provided no images get out. So, keeping up with it, she willed her power to the gadget. It turns out she only needed to push some buttons. So, she got the hang of it. Now she can't stop snapping photos of everything that interests her as she weaves through the maze.

Without warning, a hoot echoed above, and her eyes caught a giant owl swooping in faster than a camera lens. It reminded her of Capala. Speaking of the owl, her heart thumped. It should only be one of its kind. The enchantment in Talitha's room flashed in her mind.

They were the same.

Collywobbles crept up as Leviel tried to locate Talitha by ear. For precaution, she activated the doppelt. But as soon as she left her body, an invisible shield repelled her. "Ow!" Leviel banged her hands on it and backed away in reflex before she flew to the entrance. Her face smashed into an invisible shield once more. "Bloody shit!"

Closed to the gates, three men in a suit with Galen's crest advanced at a languid pace. Leviel thought they were the security. But when they neared, the coat of arms showed a book with a pen, like Evander's from the hanging tree bridge. They were from the Student Council, she assumed.

The blue-haired boy who led them took charge. "What is going on?"

Leviel reckoned his hair was natural. It was a norm for a half-fairy, half-mortal.

"I'm still assessing the premise," said a youthful red-braided-haired boy who stood on the fae's left. Unlike the others, he wore no necktie. He placed a hand on his chin as he scanned the place. His eyes, one hazel-coloured and the other a gleaming aquamarine, moved to survey the wall.

"It's enchanted," said Leviel, interjecting.

She didn't care to wait for their assessment. Afraid daybreak would come sooner before they could conclude anything. Frustrated at being kept there in place, she carried on hitting the wall. She couldn't even teleport to check the other students.

"Hitting the veil won't help," said another boy in a clean haircut, removing his coat. He tied it to his hips before pointing two fingers at his forehead. His near bloodless face and inky eyes gave him away.

An immortal, thought Leviel. But nothing came off of his attempts to break in. Too bad the rumours were true that only a handful of Gabrielle's humankind inherited her skill.

Leviel smirked. "I'm not just hitting it." She revealed the blue and green light covering her hands.

"An ersatz," said the red hair, who frowned. "No—witch."

The immortal bobbed at her. "Correction, with a witch's blood." *My father sends his regards to Lord Camdiel.*

Leviel kept trying to break the shield. *Not the place for this conversation. I will, nevertheless, relay your message.*

The immortals had their reasons for the need to hide their meetings with Lord Khycen. She, too, has reasons to keep her identity as Lady Khycen. Not that Thanatos wasn't aware of her presence. She reckoned he already knew long before she entered Galen.

"You look familiar," came a deep voice behind the immortal. The figure stepped forward, and Leviel faced the knight, now in a suit. His ivory hair would be near silver if it weren't for the ray of sun that showed its tinge of gold. In contrast to his military-cut hair yesterday, it now appeared to be a few weeks older, a tad dishevelled, and looking as if he stepped out of the shower.

What was he doing there?

"Chief!" the boys greeted.

Haniel stood toe to toe with her, oblivious to her hitting the invisible shield near his face. Her eyes locked on the crest on his coat.

Great! He leads the Student Council.

Leviel increased the powers on her hand. Why a sentinel's presence was there was beyond her comprehension. The less she knew, the better.

Still, Haniel kept his gaze fixed on her.

"Maybe you owe me in my past life." Leviel paused and batted her eyes. Of course, between them, she was the only one who lived too many lives to count. Then she went back, breaking the shield with all her anger. It gave way, hitting the sentinel right in his left eye. Taken aback, her powers seized while his helmet appeared, taking most of the brunt.

"Ow! You!" bawled Haniel.

Who told you to stand so close to me? You underestimated my powers.

Leviel teleported back to the inner maze, still barred from the outside. To her amazement, it let her through. When she turned, she found Haniel deflected by the shield. Leviel waved her hand at him. "Later," she spun and continued to track Talitha.

Leviel.

It was a voice in her head, and she froze mid-air. A force teleported her to an empty garden where a miniature palace lay on the ground. The next thing she knew, she was dwarf-like, observing the structure. Mayhap she's even smaller.

Heartbreaker, the voice called Leviel once more.

She marched inside. It was near empty, and the light from outside peeped through the upper windows. A girl in a black dress leaned on a pillar hiding from the light. Her gleaming purple eyes mirrored those of Shiphrael's. The visions of twin fireballs moving from opposite directions, meeting in the middle before exploding, flashed in her eyes.

The girl stepped into the light, and Leviel reeled.

"You're not her." Leviel's jeans and shirt morphed into a button-down, dark suit while a thick black and red cord wrapped around her arms. She stared at the golden arrow on the girl's chest, only visible to a cupid or a heartbreaker. But there's another red string. Leviel knew it did not belong to Shiphrael. It was a string meant only for a mortal.

A fire encircled the ground where Leviel stood, halting her from taking another step.

"The red chord?" the girl asked, revealing she'd read her thoughts.

Leviel nodded.

"Cut it!"

As soon as her command fell, the doors opened at the end of the gallery with a bang. A white dove popped in. Leviel espied a statue before the doors closed. The bird flew to her side and morphed into a white angel.

Chamuel. Leviel deduced and bowed. Only to do a double-take. The red string from the girl's linked with the arrow on his chest. *Adam and Eve? But why was Eve inside Shiphrael's body?*

"You've lost your mind!" said Chamuel, who never glanced at Leviel and lunged at the girl.

The girl shrugged off his hold. "You promised! They promised!"

The doors and windows of the palace shattered. Chamuel waved his hand, and the girl vanished. A sound of a church bells tintinnabulation followed. It was only then that Leviel had the archangel's full attention.

"I've let you see a joke," he said with a smile. The tintinnabulation resonated again and neared.

Chamuel peeked at the window before turning and began circling her. "You trespassed on the Kazi's mansion and witnessed the fight last night. Yet your highness left your memories untouched."

He paused as a scroll materialised, and he handed it over. The scroll contents transferred to Leviel's memory as soon as she accepted it. It was of Shiphrael, the archangel no one heard. "What am I to do with her?"

"Shh!" Chamuel placed a finger on his lips. A journal appeared. "I believe this one is what you wanted the most. The scroll is just a bonus." He took the scroll away and handed her the journal with T.K. G.'s initials. "No one has ever opened it the moment he lost his life. So none of the knights could continue investigating. Good luck."

A bribe, eh?

A bolt of lightning pierced the sky and the interiors of the palace deemed. He morphed back into his bird form. "If you need me in the future, pray."

"Why?" Leviel asked, knitting her brows. Although she already has a clue.

"I owe Sirona a great deal. And for you not to interfere with my string." Then he disappeared in an instant.

Leviel stood at the centre, trying to make sense of things. Most wanted her to cut their strings, but the archangel gave her favour to keep his. She released a breath. If she read the scroll right, the praying part that he said, was it for her or himself? Judging by his gift, the future would be bleak. Her fingers ran through the letters engraved on the journal.

A great lightning bolt struck the back door of the empty palace, making Leviel run out and stop in her tracks. Although a pile of vines cloaked a figure like a blanket, she saw through it. In front of her was a statue of a legionary angel hugging a woman.

Voices of students appeared above. Talitha was with them.

Leviel knew whoever summoned her there won't make her visible to the others.

As she neared the figure, the legionary's plain white concrete arrow morphed into gold, where the red-golden strings attached to it joined with Talitha's. Except it wasn't with the arrow lodged in her chest.

Shiphrael, Leviel thought. The strings wrapped in her arms ignited. Before she could move to test if she could break it, tiny sparkling lights wrapped around her arm.

"Halt!" said the legionary.

A moment later, Leviel witnessed a force pushing Talitha to uncover the statue covering the vines.

Right then, the journal in Leviel's hands opened, emitting chartreuse light. She wanted to break her hold on it. But a dead man's voice came out, making her freeze.

The chatterings of students within a five-mile radius besieged Leviel's ears, muting the dead while the pain in her head increased.

She tried to block them, but her powers disappeared. Then she released a string on her arm, closing the journal. The noise ceased. Leviel opened her eyes and saw Eduard sitting at the side of the fountain. A prying pressure grew on her head, and everything that happened transferred to Eduard.

Leviel gritted her teeth. "You're rude."

"Privacy isn't something we can afford in our world." He strode to her side with one hand in his trouser pocket while eyeing the journal. Leviel made it disappear. *What's on the scroll Chamuel handed?*

Leviel's eyes bugged. "You're not able to read it?"

Eduard shook his head.

"I cannot tell you. I have only changed my mind on stopping Shiphrael." She strode to the fountain and sat where Eduard vacated.

"The question is not whether you're going to stop her. It's, could you? And whether you could break the chord."

"What is the name of those figures?" Leviel asked, alluding to the statue.

"Tears in heaven."

"Why? Is it a consolation?"

Eduard studied the legionary's figure before glancing back at her.

"To commemorate Ariel's sudden struck of conscience."

"Hence its name, eh?" Leviel stood, morphing into her shirt and jeans. "It seems you have many problems on your hands. If I'm not mistaken, the being has part of Michael."

Eduard smirked. "My mission would need much of your assistance. I think meeting you is indeed a pleasure. The ones I searched for a millennium are all looking for you."

"A hazard to my occupation. I'm afraid I alone won't be enough." Leviel bowed.

The next instant, she vanished, morphed to her correct size, and teleported behind Talitha.

"She could be Nike," said Jacob, a freshman who stood among the crowd, gesturing to the female figure. The statue of Michael and Shiphrael became the centre of attraction. Despite not being on the list.

Daniel, an angel who stood opposite the mortals, sneered. "Eh? As if Michael and Nike belong to the same group."

Nike is the goddess of Victory, the daughter of Nephilim Pallas, while Michael is a heavenly Prince. The two don't fit. Daniel has a point, Talitha thought.

"Must be a sick joke," Leviel made herself visible at Talitha's side.

Talitha stopped taking pictures. She moved away so the others could have their turn. "Have you seen the rest on the list?" Talitha asked Leviel, heeling her.

"No, not yet." They exchanged brochures and checked the rest together.

An hour later, they joined the first-year students huddled inside a terrace beside the park. Most of them drank whatever cool drinks were available. Leviel misses the creydon. Out in the mortal world, she couldn't hide from the increasing heat.

Mattaniah came up to Talitha, who sat beside Leviel. He looked dapper with his light blue sapphire eyes and curly brown hair—styled in a side-swept with the ends just a tad above his nape.

Leviel gazed at the two arrows lodged in Talitha connected with those on Mattaniah's. She does not know why fate brought them together in this lifetime. They've never met before. She made sure of it. Like the golden chord, the red string destined them from the beginning, and only the almighty's order can force a heartbreaker to split it.

Cupid strings bound Leviel's right arm once more, and she reached out to test the golden rope. But she froze mid-way as Mattaniah gave her a side glance. His gleaming sapphire eyes stared her down.

One cannot harm another being without harming oneself.

Mattaniah morphed into his dark-silver chromed armour. On his breastplate the golden tree of life.

How many Michaels must I contend with?

9

General Khycen

It was a rainy afternoon following their first two classes, halting the rest. There was, however, no connection between suspending the class and the rain. And not that Leviel cared. She sat in front of the table in her room, facing the windows, enjoying a fresh pot of tea and some biscuits. The journal Chamuel handed her lay at the table.

She took a sip of her tea while her hands ran over the initials on the journal: T.K. G. If she remembered it right, none could open it. So she removed the locket from her neck, opening the latch and turning its knob until the dates changed to 9th of April 1999, at ten o'clock. To her utter surprise, the journal opened on that same date no one would expect an entry. Like any journal of a seer, the contents played like a movie:

> *Chartreuse-coloured fog surrounded the small pier as a golden-haired man unbuttoned his white shirt, showing his well-sculpted chest lying atop a wooden boat with one of his legs bent and hiding his arms behind his head. His brown matching coat and vest hung, tented on a rope that held the watercraft in place.*
>
> *A moth's eyespots distracted Tiyaniel from his absorption. Peeved by it, his eyes crossed as it hovered a few breaths from the tip of his nose. It matched the inky rims of his eyes when he wasn't brooding, unlike his almost every waking moment.*

The busy streets of Machado appeared in his thoughts once again. He was one of the most exact foretellers of his time. He knew his visions were a fact—only a matter of time.

The moth near his eyes disturbed Tiyaniel again, but he didn't blink. Without the slightest sound, he reached for its wings and saw its legs struggling while its abdomen curled. He set it free, and so did the scenes on his head.

Tiyaniel studied the cobalt sky and the moon resembling a peeping eye above the redwood trees. It added a touch of surrealism to the turquoise pool, blanketed by lotus leaves, its purple flowers, and the bright star-shaped white ones that only bloom during a full moon. Melancholy washed his soul, wanting nothing more than to return to the nixie world. He jumped off the boat, put on his vest, hooked his fingers on his coat, and slung it over his shoulders. The fog disappeared, uncovering the scattered sparks on the pond. Behind him, the moon looming larger than its usual size followed.

Next instant, Tiyaniel was now within the manor, standing at the windows, looking out. He took a sip of his glass of scotch while he observed the fireflies gathered in a sycamore tree near the pier. A pair remained above the pond, but the golden moth was no longer there. Unlike mortals, whose eyes could not catch the fireflies' quick movement, he could follow their sparks even in that distance, akin to golden string weaving a heart shape. The croak of a frog hopping to a lone lotus leaf on the water startled the pair, leaving the golden heart shape for a second before it died.

Would you have given love a chance if you were only a mere mortal?

It was a question a short girl posed to him that afternoon. Tiyaniel remembered staring at her for a moment. Those words were like a dagger stabbed into his empty soul. He does not know what it means to love someone outside his family. It has neither crossed his mind—to find love, nor the faintest idea that this girl who followed him for months has fallen for him.

After all, the girl was a cherub. A nursling. Too young to fall for him.

What is love? *Tiyaniel wondered.* Was it even worth it?

The nursling gaped at him with wide eyes, reading his mind before giving him half a smile. Another cherub appeared, and the two disappeared from his lonely manor. He hid there from then on.

Tiyaniel finished his drink and shook the memory away. As soon as he set the glass down, another vision passed through his mind. It was still the busy square of Machado but now included the silver masked monster.

Pain struck Tiyaniel's head while his heart pounded. He grasped the window frame and caught the moon's hue changed into scarlet. The glass on his hands slipped, and a ringing in his ears muted the crashing noise and replaced the cricket sounds of the night.

"Capala!"

A winged creature appeared, swooping into the closed window and landing on his arm in a blink. He hooked a miniature chest at the legs of the giant taupe-coloured owl and then caressed its head. Nostalgia struck him as he observed how rough and scaly the bird's feet were. Before, it was so tiny that it could snuggle into his palm. Now it grew over six feet tall.

Tiyaniel adored this pet. It was his only company while walking with a leash on his neck.

Tears shimmered in his eyes, for the visions answered the cherub's question.

It was never meant for him. *Tiyaniel must let go of all he cares about, including his beast. Now, Capala has to complete his last mission.*

"Remember, hand it to none other than the seraph. None other," said Tiyaniel to the beast whose wings kept brushing his face. Tiyaniel raised his arm, and the owl's feet clutched it. "See you on the other side."

The owl didn't move.

Tiyaniel supposed Capala knew his fate. He wanted nothing more than for it to stay with him, but a whistle resonated in his ears. It came still miles from the manor.

"No time to dally, my friend. Go!"

The owl left his arm and flew off. Not a moment later, Tiyaniel caught its shadow passing over the moon.

Tiyaniel, are you ready? Came a voice in his head.

"It doesn't matter." *Tiyaniel watched the broken wine glass reassemble itself and was once at the side table. He didn't come away from the window until the grandfather clock rang. It was now eleven in the evening. The owls of the mortal world in the nearby meadow quieted.*

As an ersatz, Tiyaniel has a keen sense of hearing and smell. One that made his job as the commanding knight of the Kazis—the Khycen Knights victorious.

Amid the fall, some archangels selected dead mortals to serve their cause. It brought them a second life, and since then called the ersatz. They live and breathe like mortals, but they have an angelic ability. An ersatz from the name itself meant they were only pseudo angels. They don't have wings. Their heavenly powers and attributes are only until the third generation.

Aluel was Tiyaniel's mother.

Although her lineage traces to a great sorceress, Sirona, somewhere in a twist, upon her great grandfather's death, Raphaelle selected the Selkirk's bloodline to receive the nostrum—a lifeline to the dead akin to an elixir.

Much like Lord Khycen. Except he was a conduit of her powers.

On the other hand, the Selkirk received immortality and gained angelic abilities akin to Raphaelle's.

They may not be as powerful as Lord Khycen. Still, they're the only ones that could mimic their benefactor's powers.

Raphaelle, being one of Michael's generals, made the Selkirks' existence vital to maintaining the balance between the Grigori and the Legionary army.

With his mother a Selkirk and his father a Khycen, Tiyaniel and her sister were special. However, they were the last in their family.

They have to receive enough merits to warrant another extension. Not that it was important to them. It was what the ersatzes needs.

Worse, his sister's chances are dwindling. Great beings have already placed their hands to change Leviel's fate. So, in the end, it's up to him.

Without warning, the double doors of his office flew open, and the Galen army barged in. Tiyaniel doesn't know how often he has seen this scene in his vision for almost a year.

"I apologise for the intrusion." The head of the soldiers handed him a letter. "Under Thanatos Galen's orders, you are under arrest for suspicion of treason." Then the soldier motioned for his aide to take him.

Halfway as the men grabbed him, a giant bird flew in and morphed into a knight's armour. Engraved on its teal shaded tasset was the Khycen's crest. Dark wings spread behind the armour, and Tiyaniel burst into sparks, binding with it, forming as one.

"Witch!" screech the others in the room.

Tiyaniel sneered.

"A powerful one that does not resist the order."

Nobody wanted to make the first move. And so they remained at a stalemate.

The lieutenant blinked several times, realising the head of the Kazi was indeed willing to be caught. However, he cannot go soft on him just to be sure. So, he gestured at his sergeant above.

The soldiers below stepped back while those above cast a net over Tiyaniel. In a swift, they huddled and twisted it until he could no longer budge. Tiyaniel's veins in his head throbbed, and his lungs were afire, needing oxygen to breathe. He is, in some sense, still human.

From the corner of his eyes, he saw one soldier take the mace from his wall of weaponry. He walked behind him and then struck his head.

"Again!" And on the same command repeated.

Tiyaniel stopped counting.

Mortals were brutal. Yet they have a term called 'humanity' that they lack.

Soon, Tiyaniel's legs gave out.

"Drag him out," said the lieutenant.

Not a moment later, Tiyaniel found himself dragged outside into the courtyard. His helmet, hauberk, and the net wrapped around him disappeared, but they bound his arms behind him. Two men kicked his legs, and he knelt in front of a red-robed figure seated on a chair.

"I will only ask this question once. To whom did you deliver the parcel?"

Tiyaniel raised his head, and their eyes locked briefly, then lowered. He never thought he would play hardball with this being. His father didn't have the opportunity. Not that he wished for him to be in his shoes.

"I don't know what you're talking about."

It was the truth. For only a traitor would ask that question of him. He was unaware Death would betray the order—a loophole from his vision.

"General, do you know what's at stake here?" the red figure asked as he rummaged through a black messenger bag with a yellow sticker of a chick. He drew a black journal, opened and read it. "You won't be the only one branded as a traitor. Your family will be in it too."

Tiyaniel closed his eyes. For a moment, he wanted to sway from his belief. To give in was one thing. To cross his commander was a death sentence to his race.

"I don't know what you're talking about."

"So be it," the hooded figure motioned for his men and requested a gatekeeper to open the creydon.

The clouds covered the moon while the crimson pool of blood from the lone knight thickened in the courtyard. Tiyaniel's face was no longer distinguishable.

"On your feet!" said a booming voice of a soldier near the gates. The soldiers let go of Tiyaniel's body and gathered. "FALL IN!"

"The sentinel commander arrives."

Tiyaniel heard the reverberating beat of a horse's hooves before he spotted a black chromed knight on-air swooping to his side with his white wing spread. A red plume was on his helmet, confirming his division. It disappeared as soon as he alighted. Another three followed him, but with the red plume absent from their helmet.

They were the sentinels—the real deal. They were full-bloodied angels under Michael's care as a cherub. Their order replaced the old guard that controlled the watchers before the fall. Mayhap their modern rendition, despite being centuries old. And they were far more ruthless than those stationed at Galen's forbidden ground.

"What do you mean by this, Azrael?" the sentinel commander asked, ignoring the Galen soldiers' salute, and strode to the red figure, who didn't leave his eyes from Tiyaniel's.

"When you requested the transfer and accepted the order to be here, you know I have full reign of Galen."

Before the sentinel could answer, a soldier carrying a golden box interrupted. "My Lord, we found this hidden within the volt below ground."

Azrael teleported near Tiyaniel, clamped a thick pile of his hair, and yanked his head. "Do you still deny your crime?"

Tiyaniel gnashed his teeth, not wanting to utter a single noise to satisfy the angel of death. Let alone hearing him squeal from the pain. While blood trickled into his eyes, blurring his vision, he grinned. "I am not the only one with access to it."

The red figure hated the defiance on Tiyaniel's face. He smacked his head back to the ground.

Though it didn't hurt as much as the mace, Tiyaniel lost a minute of his vision. But the ringing in his ears stopped. Small mercies, *Tiyaniel thought. His attention switched to the sentinel, whose hands now touched the golden chest before staggering, dropping the chest.*

Azrael caught the sentinel's reaction and teleported in time to see it.

"Whom did you see?"

The sentinel shook his head.

"You took an oath."

"I only answer to the Marshalls."

Azrael slapped his face.

"This is a military interrogation! Leave if you don't want to help," Azrael's scythe came out as he whirled to Tiyaniel. "Listen, young General. Your grandfather may have escaped me for the time being, but that's him. Whom do you want to go first?"

Tiyaniel felt like his head cracked and stayed silent.

"I see your sister." As soon as he spoke those words, the sleeping figure of Leviel appeared on the ground.

Meanwhile, three silver sparks of light appeared and morphed into another sentinel.

"Forgive the intrusion, your grace." Without waiting for Azrael's word, he reached for the commander's side and handed him a scroll.

Azrael swung his scythe and struck Leviel.

"No!" Tiyaniel's ropes that bound him disappeared at once. He used his remaining power to remove his sister's body from harm and flew to her.

The sentinel commander didn't see Leviel and thought Tiyaniel was rebelling.

He pulled his sword and teleported straightaway. He met Tiyaniel halfway, as they both stabbed each other on the shoulders.

"Halt!" Azrael screamed.

They both withdrew their swords.

Leviel's body disappeared while a radiating light enveloped Tiyaniel's, and lightning bolts rioted in the inky sky.

A blue light materialised beside Azrael.

"The dagger of truth," said Abdiel, in a legionary armour. He handed it to the sergeant at the side. Then gawked at Tiyaniel's blood on the ground. "It seemed this is no longer needed." Without glancing at Azrael, Abdiel took back the dagger and beamed to heaven.

The veins in Azrael's temples bulged as he eyed Haniel. "What was on the scroll?" The scroll flew to Azrael's hand before his words fell. Terror flashed in his eyes.

The heavenly sentinel walked to the fallen Kazi. He ignored the blood sticking on his lower armour as he hunched to whisper to the knight's ears. "Why?"

Tiyaniel grinned while blood spattered out from his mouth. "You know why."

"There must be another way."

"It's better to follow the order than risk the alternative," Tiyaniel's body began to disintegrate.

"It's still a life—your life!" The Commander of the Sentinels shook him. To carry out the order meant he could not let his soul roam to Azrael's territory.

"My life." He recalled the letters he received the week earlier. All retold the Khycen Knight's assassination under Thanatos's orders. "He would not stop. We ersatz are just a tool."

The sentinel stood, feeling faint. He would have never thought the General he admired was so cruel to himself. His men reached out to help him, but he flailed their arms as he leapt to his feet, closing his eyes.

"So be it." He nodded to his sergeant, who handed him his stamp and signed the scroll. "Carry out my orders!"

The sentinels pulled Tiyaniel to his knees.

"General Tiyaniel of the Khycen clan, Commander of the Knights of Kazi, I sentence you guilty of treason."

A sound of steel chains hitting the ground followed. But Tiyaniel didn't care about that. He locked his eyes with the sentinel commander, who stared back. Soon, a hood covered Tiyaniel's sight, and his shoulder grew heavier as the chains encircled his neck. Not long after, the cloth disappeared, but the sentinels' stares remained.

When Tiyaniel's face hit the ground, the golden moth settled at the tip of his nose, waiting as he took his last breath. His soul stepped off his body, and the moth flew towards him.

The moth morphed into a cherub. "If you were only a mere mortal, would you have given love a chance?" It was the female nursling from that afternoon.

It grew and morphed into a seven-year-old girl with a bobbed haircut. She was in a vermillion-coloured dress. A group of four red-orange wings appeared on her back.

"I'm sorry, General, but you can't just leave yet."

As if it sensed Leviel outside looking in, she faced her. "What is love, heartbreaker?"

Dumbstruck, Leviel snapped the latch of her locket and the journal closed. Her heart pounded, muting the pitter-patter of the rain. Leviel knew who she was.

The little girl, minus her eyes, resembled the girl that spoke to the monster in her dreams.

10

Sorrow

At fifteen seconds before the gun, Leviel was behind the starting line with several bags on her shoulders. When the horn blasted, she ran and didn't care about the laughter behind her, as she mayhap looked like a fool. She thought so too when she let her housemate talk to her about carrying their bags while they took their time.

"Lady Khycen," a young man's voice came from behind her. Leviel glanced back and found a tall, well-proportioned, bronze-skinned immortal. She knew of him from Professor Eduard's class, minus the red turban. His jet-black short brushed hair was out in the open.

"You can reach my father in the nixie world," Leviel increased her speed, but the mortal reduced their gap without an effort.

"We both know no amount of bribery from those fairies will let us through your father's ears."

She gave him a side glance and then extended her hand to him. "Call me Leviel."

"Garash." He was about to shake her hands when one bag on her shoulder slipped down her arm.

Leviel withdrew her hand. "Is this about the Council meeting?"

"Yes, and no." He averted his eyes. "I'm not reaching out to him on behalf of Lord Enki."

She raised her brows at him and then faced forward. *Mayhap he would explain why the gatekeepers were after her.*

"It's about the chest General Khycen took before his death. You haven't told your parents the truth, haven't you?"

This time it made Leviel stop and pause. Now he had her full attention.

"Listen, if the immortals stop feeding on Lady Aliya, the alternative would be the humans. A ten-mile radius of slaughter can happen in just a second." He wiped the beaded sweat on his forehead with his arm. "Annihilation may come first with the mortals. But once they're all gone, we, the immortals, would die, too. We need everyone's help on this to find a solution."

"How does this relate to the chest?"

"If Shiphrael is alive—remains alive, that is. We have a better chance of surviving. When I say us, I mean all of us. The chest must stay close and out of the Galen Army Commander's reach."

"Does your grace share the same sentiments?"

When the immortal didn't answer outright, Leviel turned and ran. Garash followed, which made her smirk. "You don't seem to be that concerned in the end. Whether she exists, your kind has to go."

"Since we've been here for a long time, we haven't found bliss. What's the point of immortality when happiness is fleeting?" Garash looked forward. "Race you to the end?"

Leviel frowned, "Are you sure you're not using your supernatural powers on this race?"

"You Kazis are not the only one who could play fair."

Long before he finished his statement, the whistle blew. "And we got ourselves a winner here. Number fifty-nine—from the House of Tobit. Followed by number ten, of Ziusudra."

They both shook hands while Garash grinned at their entwined hands. "Well, finally. Despite reversing the order." Leviel shrugged her shoulders, earning a chuckle from him. "It was a good run."

"It was. Wasn't it?" Leviel nodded. "I didn't notice the finished line."

"So did I. See you in class." Garash began his stretching.

Leviel opened a bottle. "I'd offer some, but I don't know if you—"

He shook his head.

"We do. But we better not stay too close. Not out here in the open." He gestured to the other runners that arrived. "We have an image to uphold."

"Oh, I didn't see that as a problem. When you asked for a favour." Leviel glared at him. "All right then, see you in class." She turned and saw the announcer waving at her. It was their physical education professor.

Leviel hurried to the shed, and the professor motioned the girl beside him to hand her a small box.

"Oh, thank you." When Leviel opened it, it was a gold medal with Galen's logo and a runner reaching the finished line.

"You're welcome," they said in unison.

The sound of a jeep's horn took their attention outside the open ground. Several lined olive-green vehicles parked. Men garbed in fatigues and red berets got out and stepped into the field. One lean man appeared striking in their midst, exuding a domineering aura. His board-like shoulders and back towered over the rest.

Leviel must admit, he looked exceptionally regal and aristocratic for a soldier.

She'd seen him before in one of her classes, but his bearing and clothing were far from sublime, as if he tried hard to appear ordinary.

Leviel took her eyes off him, dropped the bags and did her stretching.

Meanwhile, the professor issued orders. "Make sure everything's straight and orderly. Commander Khycen is here." He did a double-take when the officer stepped into the shed. Then stood at attention and gave the commander a sloppy salute. It was the same soldier Leviel gawked.

Leviel's ears turned red at hearing his name.

The officer didn't return his humour and narrowed his eyes while the other soldiers lined up along the sides, crowding them.

"Commander?"

"Please call me Zeus, Professor. Where are the others?"

"Mayhap asleep in their palaces." He glanced at Leviel. "Allow me to present the winner of the marathon." The officer bobbed at her, and another soldier moved to her side. He presented before her an opened velvety box where another medal lay.

"Thank you." Leviel took the box, but unlike the other, she shoved it in her bag.

"Congratulations." The commander eyed the bags on the ground. "Are these yours?"

Leviel fluttered her eyes.

The professor interjected without a thought and tapped the commander's back.

"Excusez-moi." The officer bobbed at her, and then they walked out of earshot. The soldiers at the sides scrambled away.

"Haniel," called the girl who assisted the professor earlier and walked out of the shed.

Leviel leaned over her bent knee as she watched the girl jog to the finish line to the knight, dressed in his blue running gear. Two other boys finished the race behind him, dressed in grey sweats with the Student Council's logo.

Haniel was nowhere in sight at the start of the race. Leviel stared at the clock. It seemed he caught up only several minutes behind her. *Impressive.* None of them can use their power whilst taking part in the marathon. Otherwise, they'll be disqualified. It's hard to rely on strength, especially when one has depended on their powers since birth. Hence, only several immortals were present, and angels were scarce at this event.

"Who finished first?" the braided boy from the maze asked the girl. She pointed at Leviel in response.

"You!" the boys frowned as they turned to Leviel.

"It's the one who hit the chief from the maze!" said the blue-haired boy.

Leviel took her time, bending her other knee before leaning over it. He eyed the boys for a second or two before straightening. "Hello, boys!" giving them the sweetest smile she could summon as a white cloak appeared in her hands. Then she cringed. She threw it in Haniel's direction, who caught it in his left hand. "Thomas sends his thanks."

"You're welcome," said Haniel, and the cloak disappeared.

"Oh, chief, does it mean she could hit you anytime?" the blue-haired guy asked, who approached her. "I'm Knox." He took her hand, raised it to his lips, and then let go. "I'm in charge of the first year."

"Lovely."

"Is that your name? Lovely?" he asked, grinning, knowing it wasn't so. The braided guy appeared at his side, clearing his throat. "This is Gotziel."

She bobbed at him as they shook hands.

"I'm Leviel."

"Leviel! Why does your name sound familiar?" Gotziel asked, darting his eyes over the horizon. Then to her. "Splendid name, by the way."

"Have you and the chief known long enough for him to let you borrow his cloak?" inquired Knox. It doesn't seem he wants to drop the subject at any moment. "Even Muriel there wasn't so lucky," he gestured to the girl still speaking with Haniel. "Or Jira."

Gotziel tapped her back to get her attention from Knox, "You best mind your toes, or the girls from the council will come to haunt you."

Did she hit you? Muriel asked Haniel. Her voice was loud enough for Leviel to hear while she eavesdropped. *Why does she have your cloak?*

Why, Muriel, are you jealous? At the corner of Leviel's eye, she saw a tanned girl with chestnut hair in pink running gear approaching them. Jira, she assumed.

No. Not at all, said Muriel. She glanced at Leviel, still being interviewed by the boys. *I just found the freshman intriguing. What's the deal with you and the fresh, eh?*

Leviel was not interested in Haniel's answer and turned to her matters. "Are you one of them?" Leviel eyed the hand still on her shoulders. Gotziel chuckled, withdrew his hand and raised them.

"She's a funny one," said Knox.

"Like you." Gotziel eyed him, then back to Leviel. "No. Just a warning. Those girls are not the most pleasant ones you'll come across."

"I've met my fair share."

"Not this one. You have not."

They shook their heads as they pulled her to the shed that served the refreshments.

Did you know a freshman hit Haniel in the face? Leviel heard Muriel's voice again. She searched for her and found a group of young women huddled near the table.

Indeed.

Really?

I heard she's an ersatz with a witch's ability, Muriel added.

A Khycen? A petite, tanned woman asked. She espied Leviel, who didn't look away after being caught. Leviel would rather have them know she knew they were talking about her. It was the woman who dropped her gaze first.

Impossible! One girl muttered.

Leviel no longer wanted to listen in on their talks and walked out. She took the bags from the ground before lining up for their next event.

"Wait up!" called a deep voice. Leviel didn't slow or turn. "You were eavesdropping."

"A gift since birth," said Leviel and paused. "I'm curious. What face lies behind yours now?"

"Sorry?" Haniel stared, and gone was the easiness on his face earlier.

"You heard me." Leviel gazed at him with equal seriousness. "Do you not remember me at all?"

"Oh, there you are, Haniel. You and Commander Khycen have plenty to discuss." The professor tilted his head to the officer on his side. Then he turned to the girl Leviel shared a look with earlier. "Raela, please continue monitoring the race."

"Yes, sire."

"What's your name again?" asked the commander whom Leviel hadn't noticed now stood closer to her.

"Leviel," she said, gritting her teeth.

"Khycen is not my last name. It's a namesake. You know how I got it?" he asked in a whisper.

"I'm well aware of the soldier's name who haunted the Kazi that escaped after the day your army slaughtered the knights in their headquarters," she said, gritting her teeth.

"Yet you stand there, so calmly."

"What do you have me do?"

Haniel stepped in between them. "With all due respect, sir, she's a freshman—"

"And you do not have the slightest idea who she is," he eyed Haniel, making him pause and stay where he was. The officer bent in Leviel's ears. "You have your brother's eyes."

The next instant, Leviel's powers came to life, and she hit him right on his left cheek, knocking him out.

Caught off guard, his soldiers reacted a tad too late while Haniel, who now wore his metal gauntlet, grabbed Leviel's arms. Ice materialised at once and crept into Leviel's shoulders.

A dark shadow appeared and pushed Haniel to the ground. The shadow touched Leviel's arms, and the ice melted. It was another Galen army soldier. His eyes reminded her of the demons who followed her.

Zeus got back on his feet and straightened his uniform at once. A sliced wound was on his cheeks that healed in a second.

Was the Galen soldier one of the altered creatures? Leviel thought as he stared at him, and Dr Errapel came to her mind. "So, Thanatos upgraded his dogs." She shook the water from her arms.

Her armband appeared, locking her powers. She was heedless of the soldiers gaping at her.

"I think I've changed my mind. Ersatzes aren't that bad at all."

Zeus bowed his head and left with his soldiers.

Leviel didn't take his eyes from his back and saw his feet didn't touch the ground. But none of them could see it. She knew deep in her bones he intended it for her alone. When he entered the jeep, she averted her gaze and met Haniel's scrutinising gaze. Jira was on his side. His gauntlet was still on.

"Some Chief of the student council you are."

Leviel examined her arms once more before observing Haniel's face, free of scars. *I never thought this sentinel was vain. But his cheek was free of scars as the day he was born. Angels!*

Haniel, who read her thoughts, wanted to rebut, but Jira turned his face to her. "Look at me. Stop staring at her."

Haniel froze and looked at the girl in front of him. Confusion marred his face. Then spun back once again at Leviel. But Jira pulled him. In reflex, he removed her hands from his face. "You should stop before your feelings for me go out of hand."

"No, you stop!" Jira grabbed his arm. "She's an ersatz."

"What are you talking about? So what if she is one?"

Leviel turned her back, disgust all over her face. She appeared to have ignored them and was now surveying the mountains.

"They'd never forgotten about you. Yet you do not have the faintest—"

"Stop. Not another word."

Haniel's eyes turn cold.

"Dammit! She's Leviel Khycen—the Lady Khycen. The sister of the ersatz you ordered to be killed. The one in your life before.

***

Five minutes passed midnight, and Leviel, on her teal and pink PJs, lay sprawled, sleeping horizontally on her bed with her staff animals crowding her. She hugged one sepia and plushy cream toy to her stomach. Several poundings came from her door. She tossed and turned before throwing the plushy at it. Then pulled her pillow from under her and covered her head. Still, the thumping remained.

Leviel glanced at the clock on her bedside table before throwing her blankets away. Then she marched to her door while stomping her foot. As soon as she opened the door, the singing of "Happy birthday to you...." greeted her. Her parents stood on their nightwear with a small, rounded pink and yellow cake. On top of the cake was a lit number-fifteen candle.

Camdiel took a camera out. "Go on, make a wish!"

"Do you even know how it works?" asked Aluel, moving to Leviel's side to pose. Leviel, meanwhile, closed her eyes and clasped her hands in prayer. I wished my parents would allow me to accept the mortal's scholarship, not Galen. Then Leviel blew the candle. But as the light vanished, a rumble of thunder

echoed. It brightened the inky sky for a moment before the glass windows reverberated.

"What the—" Aluel near dropped the cake and swallowed her words. Camdiel rescued the cake and stared at his wife.

Leviel could sense a vision passed on to her mother. It was an attribute of those who descended from Sirona, the greatest seer. It's also what made her brother a brilliant tactician. Her mother tells her he can foresee the future more accurately than anyone in her family.

Leviel was an exemption. She never had visions. Well, that was what they thought.

"Do you want to eat the cake or wait till morning break?" her father asked as he laid the cake on her bed and tinkered with the camera.

Leviel shook her head. "Let's all take a slice. Then save some for Tiyaniel."

"Very well." Aluel retook the cake. But Leviel grabbed it from her grasp as she went downstairs.

Her parents followed. Camdiel walked to the drawing-room and turned on his stereo. There was not a single soul leaving around their manor for miles. They needed to make sure of that. They can't have mortals wondering why their parents never aged.

She doubts her parents' attendants, housed at the servants' quarters, would mind. They weren't mortal after all.

"Hello, Aluel," came a voice, followed by a snap of yellow and green light. A silver-haired, chubby, elderly, near four feet tall that didn't even reach the back of the sofa materialised in a dark red floral dress with kind hazel eyes.

"Sirona! Right on time." Aluel strode to the elderly and hugged her, then looked at Leviel. "This is your great great-er- just call her granny."

"I'm afraid pleasantries have to wait."

Sirona glanced behind them.

"Where is Tiyaniel?"

Camdiel shared a look with Aluel, then back to Sirona. "At the headquarters." He motioned for her to sit down. "What is this about?"

"Your son is in danger. You must save him in haste!" Sirona jerked her attention to the foyer. "An Oren arrives."

Before anyone could stop her, she vanished in a jiff. Oren was their code name for a legionary angel, since their emblem often has a pine tree. When one is near, a witch would feel like their skin touched a boiling kettle.

Not long after, their front doors opened, and six men in a hood barged into the foyer, laying a casket covered in the Khycen's flag and knelt. They removed their hood, revealing their military haircut and uniform. At the sides, three sparkling lights materialised. Two of them morphed into a legionary figure. The other was a young man in a formal black suit fit for mourning.

Leviel looked at the casket covered with the Khycen flag. As if hypnotised, her legs carried her closed to it. She slid the flag to the ground and used her powers to open it without preamble.

Tiyaniel's lifeless face greeted her.

The stereo and every glass at the manor exploded. Leviel didn't know who did it. It could be her or any of her parents. Without a thought, she waved her hand, and the cheap enchantment on Tiyaniel's face vanished, and his mangled face appeared.

Leviel's mouth opened as she looked above and watched as the chandelier fell. With arms wrapped around her, she disappeared out of the way while her brother's casket slid off. The chandelier splattered on the ground and shattered a second time.

Leviel reappeared at the entrance while struggling in her saviour's arms—the young man in a suit. She scratched his face, wanting him to let her go. Only when blood trickled out of his wounds did Leviel stop.

The howling quieted. It was then she realised it was she and everything was her doing. The stereo, the glasses, and the chandelier were because of her screams. Yet she heard none of it. Soon she wept.

Stern, teal-coloured eyes captured hers, morphing into silver eyes she'd always know whom it belonged to. "Piuthar." Sister. A dead man's voice came as if he whispered in her ears. "Tell *our father to stay away from the Galen army and not trust anyone, especially Zeus."*

Leviel quieted as she thought, Why would Tiyaniel hide his message in this young man's eyes? Before she could probe further, a scene appeared in her head:

> *"General Tiyaniel of the Khycen clan, Commander of the Knights of Kazi. I sentence you guilty of treason," said the same young man who held her in his arms.*
>
> *Tiyaniel's horrifying death flashed in Leviel's eyes as if she was Tiyaniel himself, cloaked in a hood and choked to death.*

The howls of her parents soon jolted her, and she returned to reality. She realised that when the man forced the casket out of the falling chandelier, it slid towards her parents. Now she could only watch as they hugged Tiyaniel's body covered with holes.

Soon, the tears on her face dried, and she turned to the young man holding her. "Murderer!" Leviel knocked her head to his face with force, and his hold loosened. She slapped, scratched him again, and choked him with all her might. "You killed him! You are a murderer!"

"Leviel!" she heard her father's call before she felt a blow strike her head. Darkness engulfed her at once.

> *A Kazi in his glorious armour appeared. "Did you have a delightful dream?"*
>
> *"No. I had a nightmare," said Leviel, who outed.*
>
> *The Kazi smiled before his bloodied face inside the coffin entered her view, and Leviel screamed.*

When she opened her eyes again, she saw herself dressed in black, standing at the Kazi's cemetery, where only a huge white moon lit their way.

11

Face-off

$\mathcal{L}$eviel found the breakfast buffet tolerable and boring. Not even the Khycen's greatest enemy, Thanatos Galen, was enough to make her excited. Although, a great being appeared briefly, arresting time as if its powers couldn't stop it from doing so. She would have been oblivious had it not been for her scalding armband, prepping her to be on her toes and the sudden absence of the ticking noise of the clock hidden on her locket. Too bad she could use its presence to liven the course.

Her spirits soared when Chamuel and Thanatos departed half an hour later. Though not in a positive sense. Finding them together on good terms made her unsettled.

It put her back at zero on her quest, and she was now sceptical regarding Tiyaniel's journal.

When Leviel lost sight of them, she eyed the people on her table, and in a blink, she activated the doppelt. Not long after, Leviel appeared outside the venue.

Two cars stopped in the driveway. One had the Shuruppak's coat of arms, while the other had Thanatos'. Leviel cringed as she saw the two archangels get inside the car. Regarding pretences, Thanatos is the master. *No doubt about it.*

Lady Aliya appeared after they left and ordered her aide to chase Thanatos' car as Leviel pondered how to follow them without being too obvious.

Brilliant! She teleported inside the vehicle and sat beside the clueless Princess, whom she checked from head to toe.

Aliya's looks are indeed uncanny, resembling too much of Shiphrael.

When they reached the university's entrance, to Leviel's utter surprise, the immortal ordered the driver to carry on following the other car through the gates.

Her eyes darted to the stones in Aliya's palm. *How did she get those?* Only a tracker could possess and sanctioned to use them. It involves the cadre's proxies and, therefore, must be dealt with by stealth. Leviel knew of only one division those trackers belonged to, Michael's Legionary Army. It requires a superior rank to get it outside of the capital. *Like an archangel, perhaps.* Not that she's aware that anyone other than with Michael's rank could. But she doubts it was Gabrielle. The archangel didn't need it.

Aliya and the driver's talks diverted her absorption. It took a while for her to understand the drift. Leviel turned worried when the Princess traipsed into the forbidden ground.

She'd gone marbles! Didn't she realise it was one of the most well-guarded places in all realms? A scraping sound from the fence made Leviel gaze up. *They weren't statues at all.* Atop the wall, dozens of hooded seven-foot-tall sentinels moved into a readied position to shoot an arrow facing Aliya.

Their tattooed forehead was now out of the open. Aliya should know they were the ancient sentinels if she'd listened during Professor Eduard's class. Their only task after the fall was to guard the forbidden ground.

Since Leviel was in a doppelt mode, she had to remain a bystander. She wasn't a fool to give herself away, to save an unruly immortal. Also, Aliya is impeding her intentions. She went there to enquire, not to alert them.

The sentinel closest to the gate jumped. Its thud was a chain-like noise hitting the ground. Then he released his arrow. With lightning speed, Leviel teleported to Aliya's side and deflected it before it struck her. She winced, discomfited for revealing her presence. Leviel thought he'd give her just a warning shot.

Killing Aliya there wouldn't bode well for everyone. The sentinels are way off the loop.

Aliya ran back and got inside the limo while the sentinel shot several more.

SHIT! The fool didn't stop targeting Aliya.

Leviel advanced to stop his arrows, but her legs felt like logs. She saw a pair of arms sprouted from the ground while its hands clamped her legs. Leviel tried to move, but it kept her in place. Left with no choice, she made herself visible and scanned her surroundings.

An onyx-eyed soldier from earlier who melted Haniel's ice on her arms stood behind her. He was shaking his head, giving her a silent warning while they watched as the sentinel chased after the Shuruppak's limo. When it was out of sight, the soldier passed by.

"Can you let me go?" Leviel struggled from the hold while trying to use her powers to break the grip.

The soldier didn't pause and carried on leaving her.

"When are you going to release me?"

He didn't look back.

"You can't just leave me here! I have other matters to attend to!" She summoned her powers again, but the hands didn't budge. Rage filled her, and her armband disappeared at once as her sorcerers' blood came to life. "Leig leam falbh!"

The hands unclasped her legs, retreated down, and the hole in the ground vanished. Her armband materialised again, halting her powers. Dissatisfied with the soldier, she ran after him. Only to find too late that her legs numbed, and she stumbled. "Ow!" She flinched as she pinched her lower muscles.

A steel thud above the fence startled her. The sentinel who chased the immortal's limo tucked its arrows behind him while sedimentary dust fell from his body. He lined himself with the rest, still in the position to shoot. Then they moved at attention in synchrony. In the next second, they appeared, cloaked and unmoving as any other statue.

"Guten tag. I'm Leviel." She approached the leader. As someone who had studied their formation, she knew their captain stood at the centre—the old guard. "I'm the late General Khycen's sister."

Tiyaniel's diary appeared in the air and sailed to the sentinel.

The old guard's hood lowered, but his head was still a statue.

"I came for you. According to Tiyaniel's journal, his owl, Capala, should have passed here the night he died. The owl was supposed to deliver a parcel. Do you know to whom? Or why it returned to the headquarters?"

The sentinel jumped off the fence, and the ground cracked at its impact while Leviel wobbled. She found his towering height, which was near twice as the others intimidating and felt sudden cold feet. Leviel took a few steps back, but the sentinel grabbed her. The old guard morphed into its mortal form, a ruddy and youthful man, full of smiles with jet black hair, then withdrew his hand. A gold ring was around his head to keep his hair from crowding his face.

"Did you say an owl?"

"Yes. Brown-grey coloured and has a heart-shaped face. An owl in the nixie world. It was four years ago." She opened her palm, showing an image of Capala like a projector.

"The red moon?"

Leviel nodded, remembering Tiyaniel mentioned the scarlet hue of the moon.

"An archangel appeared here and met the owl." Without preamble, he teleported Leviel to the fence. He pointed at the barren portion of the park. "There. I remembered the purple light well. It was akin to the eighth."

By the eighth, he meant Shiphrael's.

"Are you sure?"

The sentinel nodded.

Leviel's brows furrowed. "Was it, by any chance, a seraph?"

"It could be it too," the sentinel frowned back at her. Shiphrael was part seraph, a part archangel. "Though it didn't show any hint of fire then. It appeared to be a cherub."

Leviel shook her head. "Any of the Princes?" The visions from the ruined manor implied that Capala had to meet one of the heavenly commanders.

"No, they don't use these gates," the sentinel teleported her back to the ground while he remained atop the fence. "Where's the owl now?"

"Dead, frozen—I'm not sure. It died in my arms but lingered on the Kazi's HQ."

"Mayhap, talk to it," he batted his eyes at her, raising his brows while grinning.

Leviel scratched her head and cracked up. She'd never thought of it.

"What's your name?"

"Milo."

"It was nice meeting you, Milo. Thanks for the gen," Leviel waved at him.

"You're welcome," he bobbed. Then his hood was up, and he was a lifeless stone again.

Leviel strolled away from the road leading to the forbidden ground. She turned to an alley flanked by high-walled fences, barring the overgrown ginkgo trees on the side of the street. Immersed with Milo's information, she was oblivious to the falling leaves doubling as she passed. A ticking sound made her pause and glanced at her locket.

She unfastened the latch and saw the clock turning fast forward. Then, a white feather fell, covering the timepiece. Leviel gazed up and saw the feathers raining along with the amber leaves. She backed away at breathtaking speed, avoiding the spear-shaped ice that flew in her direction. Several minute versions of it chased her, sparing her no time to breathe.

Leviel hurried herself to a wall, kicked her legs and hurled herself in the air. She escaped only a second before they struck the wall. Sensing more to come, Leviel activated another doppelt mode, making two clones of herself. She hoped her other clone at the breakfast buffet was back at their manor, and no one witnessed it disappear.

Without warning, five gatekeepers materialised above her.

She teleported away, letting her clones scramble in opposite paths to distract them. To her horror, a shield arrested her flight, realising now they sealed the alley.

Leviel landed with her hands fisted at her sides as she shook her head. She accepts her defeat and lets her clones disappear, braving the gatekeepers. "What is it you want?"

"The locket," said the only female among them, who paused several paces away from her. Two other gatekeepers hovered above Leviel while a pair guarded each exit point. "There is no way out."

I can see that.

The angel extended her hand to Leviel. "Now, Lady Khycen, if you please, hand over the timepiece."

Leviel shook her head. "Her grace gifted this to me on my first birthday." *My very first life.* Raphaelle placed it on her neck on the day she was born. It remained with her no matter how many lives she had. "I shall return it to her if she asks of it."

"To which, her grace, Gabrielle lent to Raphaelle. She only wants it back."

Leviel smirked. "You meant she would no longer follow the bargain of letting Shiphrael be reborn. And I too." She clamped the locket. Then she tugged it off until the necklace broke.

The female gatekeeper advanced, but Leviel felt her pry her mind open.

"Halt!" Leviel raised her hand. "Why are you trying to open my mind?"

"Her grace wants a favour?"

"Blimey! Is this how you ask a favour?" Leviel raised a brow. "Don't tell me she too wanted me to break off someone's chord. If it's hers, there will be no problem."

The gatekeeper shook her head. "I'm afraid it's much harder than her own heart."

Does she even have one?

Her rebut earned a painful prick in her temples.

Though unsolicited, she understood a lot after Chamuel's filling her in on Shiphrael.

"Still, it doesn't explain why you're trying to invade my mind." Because Leviel would cut the cord that bound Michael to Shiphrael, it was her mission.

"This is not a child's play. You need all the help." The gatekeeper increased the onslaught of her mind. The two others above her attacked.

Leviel could not hold off the pain and the tattoo on her arm ignited, a sign her mother's blood reawakened. She wasn't a fool to let a gatekeeper control her. The two gatekeepers cried as crimson tears streamed down their eyes as soon as they touched her. In the next second, they let go. But the gatekeeper on the north exit took the pendant from Leviel's hand.

The cream-cloaked Kazi from the ruined manor came out of it. She slashed the gatekeeper's limbs and, at a rapid pace, sliced the legs of the female angel who still had the power over Leviel's mind.

"You," said the female gatekeeper at the Kazi. "You shouldn't exist here."

"I'm a part of her. You can't kill me." The Kazi turned to avoid another attack. Then ran to Leviel, who stood rooted, watching a giant glacier falling on her. "Move!"

A force pulled Leviel away only to face the silvery-eyed monster from her dreams, appearing more real than ever.

She blinked and found it gone. It materialised behind her, blocking her from a whirlpool of feathers.

Feathers to a mortal's eye, that is.

Angels knew Gabrielle's weapon—a plume-shaped blade sharped enough to cut a diamond. Worse, once cut, no matter how tiny the wound, it will freeze its victim's entire body in an instant.

On that note, Leviel's jaw dropped as she watched the beast open its humongous mouth, swallow them like candies, and remain unscathed.

"Another creature that shouldn't exist here!" said the gatekeeper, who regained her legs, assisted by the others. "This shall not end well, Heart—"

A gigantic tongue smacked and wrapped her with the others before her words could fall, then rolled back to the monster's mouth. The beast chewed them well, oblivious to the crimson liquid dripping from its mouth. Bolts of rioting blue lightning swirled past them. Mattaniah Evander materialised in its midst, making the monster choke a finger before carrying on.

"Oh, there you are."

Mattaniah sent a mammoth-sized granite stone to the monster, who remained rooted as the rock broke into pieces. A blue light came out of the monster's mouth and shot at Leviel's chest.

She gazed down and saw the locket was now back, hanging on her neck. Leviel looked back at the beast, who stared at her, pulling her into his thoughts. It conjured two images into her vision:

Sanguine driblets from scratches on a porcelain face she knew it was her doing before it changed into a botched face of a fallen knight who called her Piuthar on her fifteenth birthday.

Without warning, a knight in black chrome armour appeared behind the monster, destroying its hypnosis on her. His helmet had a red plume and matched the image of a Sentinel Commander. He charged the beast with his sword, which vanished instantly. Leviel faced it instead. But the Kazi from the manor appeared, taking the onslaught. Her hooded cloak fell open, revealing a silver-eyed, raven-haired girl Leviel knew as the dead Lady Leviel Khycen.

Her eyes welled, staring back at the Kazi, who grew paler by the second. She was her wandering soul.

It burst into several golden moths and entered Leviel's forehead, and the clock within her locket turned rapidly counterclockwise, arresting time within the mortal world.

The scenes of her in a Kazi armour flashed in her mind, where lightning danced above before heaven opened. A horde of grey sentinels sailed down as they rode their horses. At the front was a black chromed knight with a red plume in his helmet. It was the same armour Haniel wore at the meadow. Then the scene switched to a beautiful young girl with an infant in her arms. A sentinel grabbed the child away from the girl. Lady Leviel, at the sides, interjected between them, meeting the dark knight's sword in return. Scarlett-coloured liquid splattered from Leviel's chest as she looked at the shaken, teal-coloured eyes of the sentinel commander.

The next instant, the scene switched to the day when Haniel and his men stepped into the portal after delivering Tiyaniel's casket. It burst and went up into flames. Not long after, a tiny fiery cherub materialised. It collected the debris into a bottle. When she turned, Leviel saw the girl with bobbed hair—the same girl from Tiyaniel's journal. She was smiling. Instead of having the same silver eyes as hers, it was a beaded onyx.

Leviel's visions died as if a mirror shattered into pieces.

Meanwhile, the dark chrome knight, still frozen, morphed into his usual black suit student council uniform, revealing himself as Haniel. The cherub stepped out of the broken mirror into the present, looking at him. Haniel floated in the air, snapping back like a sling, stretched to its limit. With a flick of her finger, his chest opened. Hundreds of butterflies flew out.

Is she collecting his soul once more? Leviel wondered. But before she could conclude, the ground she stood shook. She fell from a portal before pausing mid-air. Down below, the structures of Galen crumbled, and the flaming sky readied to swallow the world.

The opened locket came into Leviel's view. On instinct, she snapped it closed, and everything arranged itself like a puzzle.

Golden moths came flying out of Leviel's forehead. It was once again like it was. The gatekeepers and their frost disappeared while she stood on the ground facing Haniel. Eduard Galen, with the House of Mikhail's angels, stepped inside the veil. They crowded behind Evanders, who witnessed everything at the sides.

Knox and Gotziel also arrived and flanked Haniel, who now awoke. He withdrew his sword, and it faded. He clamped his arm on Leviel.

"I suggest you keep your wig on," he said in a whisper. "For I remember you now, heartbreaker. The question is, do you?"

With only the ginkgo leaves falling above them, Leviel used her vision as the heartbreaker.

Lodged in Haniel's chest was a golden arrow with a missing tail. Unlike any other beings whose strings she cut into half to separate their fate and feelings, his arrow never bloomed. It was an act only she—the heartbreaker could achieve.

A gust of wind passed, and several students in a suit with the Selkirk emblem lined behind Leviel. They were senior students of Galen, she assumed. It was a requisite for those in their final year and those who sat as council members to dress in formal wear.

Before Leviel could discern their intention, Foliel appeared at her right out of the blue.

"Lord Khycen sends his message to the sentinels: You have reached your limit." He pulled Leviel from Haniel's grasp.

Startled at the ersatzes unified front, Haniel dropped his hold.

Mattaniah bobbed his head to Foliel before meeting Leviel's eyes.

She knew full well who runs the show.

"If Gabrielle wishes to interfere, she risks waging war with Raphaelle. I say it as Lady Khycen, new head to the Kazis." Leviel bobbed at Eduard, then at Haniel, who turned pale by how she addressed herself. Without waiting for Mattaniah's answer, she raised her hands. "Go!"

The Selkirks with the Khycens vanished.

12
Raguelle

The ersatzes arrived at the amphitheatre between two hills, where a band played a rock song. Leviel noticed the Selkirks were now sporting random, casual wear to match the other students in the festival. She and Foniel were out of place. Leviel morphed into her shirt and jeans, motioning for him to do the same. Then she turned her attention to the ersatzes once more.

Their show of solidarity back at the alley did not awe her. They appeared to her rescue when the fight was over. *With only a lone sentinel to deal with, why couldn't they come sooner? Haniel was a fly to her. He was harmless for now.*

"Did my father send you here to babysit?" She glanced at Foniel.

"A parent couldn't sit still and watch their remaining child walk to the lion's den without aid." Foniel shrugged his shoulder. "Of course, that's my humble opinion. They order. I follow."

Leviel forgot that although he appeared meek at her father's office, Foniel was far from a sheep. She must stop this conversation before his tirade began. Apart from his administrative position, he was one of her father's shadow guards and had taught her defence art throughout her lifetime. So, he took it upon himself to act as her uncle and say the words Camdiel withheld. It also meant his on Camdiel's side. *Not hers—all the time.*

"May I say, my lady, that this isn't the wisest—"

Leviel spotted Sybil and her friends seated further to the back and waved at them to dismiss him. They gawked at her, making

Foniel take a pause. Given the scale of the space and the crowd, one may need a telescope to spot them. It took a minute or two before Sybil waved back while Foniel recovered his thoughts.

"—decision—I don't think the witches like you. Not the slightest bit. And vis-à-vis," he said with one raised brow, letting her know that her attempts to deter him didn't go unnoticed.

"What are you talking about? She's my cousin. The Selkirk's know her." Leviel plastered a smile as she waved again.

Nariel, who sat close to her, nodded. But Foniel frowned. "You would rather look like a fool to a stranger than listen to me."

Nariel burst out laughing, making Leviel's face darken.

Go away.

"I know when I'm not welcome anymore."

Foniel disappeared.

"You realise many of us care for you, don't you? It's just that your family is unwilling to accept a helping hand." Nariel clapped as the song ended and didn't glance at her.

The Selkirks were Sirona's direct relatives. But Thanatos does not hate them as much as the Khycen clan.

Even now, they remained unscathed by his anti-Kazi movements.

Leviel assumed that since the angelic army lost a leg when the Galen soldiers slaughtered the Khycen Knights, moving the Selkirks would touch Raphaelle's bottom line.

Thanatos wouldn't dare go against her.

Among Michael's quadrate of archangels he used as a scheme during the great battle, Gabrielle isn't the one to be feared then. It was Raphaelle. She took care of the Grigori's commander all by herself.

"To embroil yourselves with this web meant you entangle yourselves on a bloody cause I don't know for whom or for what." She did not want the Selkirks to suffer the Khycen's fate. So their gap was necessary. "I do, however, need to fulfil my mission, which I hope would involve none of my family."

"This next song is from Knight to his damsel in distress. Damsel, whomever you are, I hope you are listening to this song."

Leviel eyed the singer of the band. She heard the girls talking about Evander calling Talitha the same thing. Then, out of the blue, she teleported into a massive tent.

"It'll rain," said Nariel while a clap of thunder rumbled. Then came the sound of pitter patter.

"My thanks, then." Leviel looked at the downpour outside the tent's entrance. She noticed the rest of the Selkirks from earlier were with them. *I supposed it was an advantage of being a family of seers.*

One of them got some drinks from the bar and distributed them. "What's your poison? I'm Nadiel, Nariel's sister."

"Cousin," Leviel grabbed a beer bottle and raised it to her. "Thanks."

Their group discussed the possibility of the witches resisting the immortals, more so in Sirona. If she jumped ship, it wouldn't be pleasant for their family. The Selkirks were neutral but could not stand idle, leaving their non-ersatz relative at the immortals' mercy.

Leviel believed that was a downside of being an ersatz.

They have non-angelic relatives, unlike their purebred counterparts, who only have to consider the archangel they serve, more like the Khycen, who would always follow Raphaelle's stand.

Not long after, the tent crowded. Leviel saw Talitha, Tirzah and Sybil and had them join her peers.

After the introductions, the Selkirks changed the topics and made it more mortal accommodating.

Zeus and several of his men neared them, and it didn't go unheeded by Leviel. Regardless of his power, her gut feeling would spot her enemy no matter where it hides. Perhaps, also aided by her life's mission. He stood beside her and handed Talitha a cocktail glass from a tray behind her.

"Thanks!"

"My pleasure. I'm Zeus." He gave her a brilliant smile while Leviel rolled her eyes.

"Talitha," she said, smiling back at him.

Leviel interjected between them while they shook hands. "Leviel from House of Tobit." She fixed Talitha a look. *You're shaking a wolf's hands, little girl.* When Talitha didn't react, she darted her eyes to Zeus, who shook her hands too.

She can't hear you, he said via Telepathy.

Your doing? No, don't answer that.

Zeus grinned and then introduced the men with him to the others. *Had it been the Khycen knight with her, would it be the same story?* She noticed the onyx soldier wasn't present. "Where's your shadow guard? I have yet to thank him for saving me once more." *And also to give him a piece of my mind from stopping me at the Forbidden grounds.*

"Not everyone appreciates being called a dog," referring to her sarcastic remark earlier that morning. Zeus nudged his head to the back of the tent, where his guard held an unopened beer bottle. He noticed them staring and raised it to them. "You can call him Zev. That's his name for now." Then he chuckled. "Why? Did you miss him? I can lone him to you if you like. Although, I can't promise you he won't bite."

Leviel glanced at the crowded bar and then waved her hand. The two mortals who sat in the middle moved to the sides. She pointed at the empty stools. "There are some important matters we need to discuss. If you please, Commander Khycen."

"Oh? I don't recall we have anything to discuss. If we have a date, this won't be it.

"Funny. A cherub in bob hair, eyes as dead as your guard and dresses in the colour of fire—the eighth's fire. Does it ring a bell?"

Zeus took a sip of his beer before grinning and saying, "I'm all ears." Though he said that, he spoke at length while she listened.

He shares that she's called the angel Raguelle. But it wasn't straightforward as the others. She was akin to Shiphrael but did not wield as much fire as her. She's considered a seraph. Though, unlike Shiphrael, created with equal parts and from the highest feather class, Raguelle's feathers do not belong to the top seraphim. With only four wings, she was more of an archangel that wields less power at the court and in its truest sense.

Despite it, the monster was under the little girl's control. None of the cadres could. Zeus believed it to be the second apocalypse.

Should it evolve, it would wipe out Michael's entire legionary armies. It was a backup plan should Shiphrael could not do as destiny decrees or if she seized control of Michael's powers. Worst, fail a second awakening.

"So, you believe she would?"

"It's only a matter of time. Why do you think you received such an order? And why are you here, heartbreaker?"

"You. I am here because of you." Leviel rolled her eyes and shook her head. It earned a grin from Zeus, who now has five empty pints and three shot glasses. Leviel threw another shot at the back of her throat, then gave him a side glance. "Why am I dreaming of her and the monster?"

"I don't know." He shook his head and rubbed his temples. "Why is this mortal's body so weak?"

Leviel observed his ruddy face and knitting brows.

"Alcohol does that to mortals. Mayhap because when you fell off, it took all your energy." Her mind conjured an image of him gliding down from heaven, wings turning dark before breaking into pieces and landing straight on the ground. Or water.

"Don't let your imagination run wild. It didn't happen that way."

"Oh, care to share how it went?"

He shook his head. "Another time."

"I assume you don't know everything. Then why don't you give me your best guess why Raguelle and this monster—"

"You might be the only one who could stop them." He looked more severe than ever. "Or help them achieve their cause." His answer stopped Leviel midway from drinking her beer. "My best guess is the former."

If the omens were exact, then what Zeus said makes sense. "Either way, you need me to be on your boat. Too bad you were Tiyaniel's only concern, not Thanatos Galen."

"Don't let Azrael hear you say that," Zeus gestured to his men and stood. "I don't think his purpose was to kill him in the end." He raised his hand to stop her from speaking. "The sentinel made his conclusion, and it turned for the worst. You're here in his backyard, and he has yet to harm you. Azrael's greed for the chest will not be dealt with. At least, not by me. Samael—the real keeper-er-theft of that soul. That is his responsibility."

"How very lucky for the Khycen to take the brunt," Leviel gave him a lopsided grin. "Thanatos' concerns border like an obsession. How much of Shiphrael's life force did he gather? I bet you don't know." She watched as Zeus's eyes darkened. "Whose soul is it… hidden in the chest, then?" She stood toe to toe with him while her eyes darted to Talitha. "I wish to return what you'd taken from her."

"You need to open the chest to find out, heartbreaker." He placed a black card at the bar and turned before pausing. "You, more than anyone else, need what's hidden there to complete your mission. I don't—not anymore. Not that I wish to help you. Far from it."

"What a waste of Tiyaniel's life."

Zeus' face turned ruddier than before as he glanced behind Leviel.

At the far corner of the tent, Talitha danced with a mortal. *Nathan, is it?* She can't remember the young man's name. When she glanced back at Zeus, she placed him on her cupid dominion and found his chest devoid of a heart, confirming her theory.

"Enjoy the rest of the evening," he said, breaking her cupid hold, and with his men, he strode out of the tent.

Upon his departure, the Selkirk approached her. Nariel eyed the exit, watching Zeus' back. "It seems tomorrow would be a bloody day."

"Shit will fly!" said another Selkirk.

"God help us all."

"Crimson."

The rest cursed and shared their version of what tomorrow would hold.

"Even more reason to enjoy the night." Nadiel jigged with her fist and twirled. The music pumped out louder than before.

As her peers carried on, Leviel fixed her gaze on Talitha, who morphed into a girl under a tree, looking at several large white birds with hearts hanging on their beaks. But she could only watch them and never dare reach out for one. The illusion disappeared as if on a smoke screen.

Leviel blinked.

Talitha stepped away from Nathan's reach. She grabbed Tirzah along the way, who held Sybil, and off they went.

Leviel cracked up, and Nadiel gave her a questioning look. She sobered right away. "Say, would you be able to wipe all of Zeus's men tonight?" The Selkirk all froze. "In theory?"

"I stationed a battalion just outside the city," said Nariel.

"You're well prepared." Leviel walked backwards. "Maybe next time." She raised her two fingers to her forehead and gave them a sloppy salute before turning to the exit. Although the Selkirks were a formidable army, they lacked the military discipline and gambit embedded in the Khycen's DNA.

Leviel burped twice and cursed at the drinks.

When she was outside, scattered students, looking out of their trees, filled the empty benches. She found the lane of golf cars from earlier devoid of it. Hence, it explains why they're still there. As she strode to the small gate, she felt a little tipsy. She near crashed into a post but steered away before the impact, making her recover her bearings. Close to her, Leviel spotted her housemates in the same predicament. Talitha looked worst among the three, throwing up at a bin. To her surprise, Zeus was also at the side, drinking from a water bottle.

I thought you left. Leviel eyed him, then scanned the beaming faces of her mates. "Girls!" She bobbed while her eyes fixed on the man, who appeared nonchalant. *Couldn't you offer some gallantry and send them home?*

What? Why should I blow off my cover for its sake? No, thank you. I'll trouble you then, Lady Khycen. Zeus hid his grin by taking another sip of water.

Oh, it's Lady Khycen now. Chivalry is indeed dead.

He chuckled. *Oh, wasn't benevolence part of your trait as an ersatz? I'm only a part of him, and it's not one of the attractive traits I've acquired.*

Only the mean part. Leviel smirked and released a sigh as she glanced at her housemates. "I'll bring you home, but only two at a time." She eyed Talitha, who kept gagging at the front of the bin. Then turned to Zeus. *Oi, I leave her to you, gentleman or not. Enjoy your time. I'm sure you would appreciate this small* favour. There won't be another. Under different circumstances, I would take her far from you.

Without preamble, she grabbed Tirzah and Sybil and teleported them to the manor. She deposited them in the drawing-room. They were old enough to drink. They should manage a flight of stairs. Suddenly she felt her locket open, and the clock turned counterclockwise again.

I'm sure in demand.

Leviel disappeared at once from the manor. She had been jumping from one tower to another for half an hour when the clock's turn halted as if it had stopped working. Leviel scanned her surroundings and realised she was at the centre of a lit beech tree tunnel near the House of Adams.

She closed her locket and heard a nearing noise from the opposite end. A little girl in a fiery-coloured dress materialised and strolled to her. Her onyx eyes turned amber, matching the lamps on the trees' boughs.

Without warning, a powerful vision pulled Leviel's thoughts to when Tiyaniel's soul stood at his corpse.

> *"I'm sorry General, but you can't just leave yet," said Raguelle to Tiyaniel before she opened her palm, sucking in his soul.*
>
> *A burst of golden moths emerged from her other palm, transforming into a behemoth reptile. It had several limbs and a humongous mouth. One could mistake it for an octopus if it weren't for its scales.*

In a blink, the scene disappeared. Raguelle smiled at Leviel, with eyes forming half a crest. "Whether Tiyaniel remains alive is in your hands. Now, you can decide which ship to board." Her fiery wings came out and left Leviel quivering on her knees.

Thousands of golden moths whirled around Leviel, making her faint before darkness took her.

13

Respite

After the tree incident, a truce from all sides seems to have occurred. The gatekeepers have not bothered Leviel again.

It gave her time to relish the twenty-minute walk to the university grounds. Not that she didn't give in to teleporting when laziness arises. She delighted in watching the trees, birds, and cherubs atop the towers with the other girls.

For a moment, she can breathe despite her nemesis and other dangerous beings within arm's length. She has yet to cross paths with Thanatos again.

She also had the chance to study Talitha in depth. Although it's her body, she's non-existent. Her every waking moment and thought is Shiphrael's. It only meant Shiphrael's soul broke in two. One stripped with her memory while the other has it with all its anger.

If she based it on the tree incident, Shiphrael kept her seraphim powers, but not Michael's. Then it would mean the key is the life force taken during her incineration.

Still, the great dilemma is that if Talitha regains her body, what would happen to Shiphrael's broken souls? Not to mention that someone inhabited the archangel's body. It explains why Thanatos is hunting for her life force and Talitha's soul. They didn't think things would get graver when they disposed of Shiphrael. It serves them right.

Leviel would never wish to be in his or the cadre's shoes. She's pretty satisfied by the sluggishness of her life now.

It may be subdued and slow in contrast to her previous lives. Still, there were more than a dozen matchmakings Leviel needed to undo from the cherubs' naughty target practice. It's the reason she least enjoyed going to Professor Stephanie Singh's class. Not everyone knew she was the heartbreaker cupid, and listening to Singh encourage the students to find their one true love made her occupation harder. False entanglement was one thing. But a web was a year's worth of headache.

Leviel wasn't as unfeeling as history talks of the heartbreaker cupid. If she could spare the world of heartache, she would. Love and hate, however, were always intertwined. One can grow in the other's absence.

This temporary respite also meant she didn't get more answers from Khycen's old HQ. Thanatos had up the ante in his security, and she wasn't ready to give Zeus an answer.

She supposed she wasn't the only one biding her time.

To say the matter was delicate is a complete understatement. None could outright choose whom to side with.

On the one hand, Raguelle is only a mere angel. But her powers are beyond an archangel. So whoever was pulling her string—no doubt even Lucifer and Michael combined could not stop her. The question is, are they even doing anything about it?

On the other, it'll be mayhem. Three different forces could not decide whether to join hands or fight, making this arduous. All of which have their vendetta.

To spare herself the headache, Leviel focused on her student life. She pushed the problem to the back of her mind. She embraced the winter exam and lounged at the library like the mortals. It helped keep her mind off it and sped up life a bit. Eduard had grilled them—perhaps way overboard. Enough that even she scrambled for answers. He lost many fans and gained haters. Not that it mattered to a warrior like him.

When Christmas break came, Leviel was the most cheery in contrast to the rest, whose mood plummeted at their temporary parting. It meant she could now attend the House of Tobit party. Over her lifetime, she was busy watching over Shiphrael and untangling hearts. She'd never had the chance to be at Tobit's glamorous parties. Only through Thomas' eyes. She won't miss this chance.

Too bad for Tirzah, who wanted to stay for the break, but her mother arrived yesterday to pick her up. Leviel still sees the same displeasure on her face. She reckons nothing pleases her. For a moment, Leviel assumed Tirzah had grown some backbones over the months. In the end, she didn't even voice her sentiment. At least not in front of her mother.

The night before, Tirzah kept pestering them as if they'd made a mistake about Ezri, their defence arts professor. Leviel knew whose proxy he was. It's best not to entangle with him. The brunt, of course, lay on Talitha, for she was the only witness.

Leviel felt complicated about Tirzah from the beginning and only worsened as time passed. Her instincts tell her there was something off about her. But she couldn't pinpoint a thing as she could not read through her.

Now out there in frigid weather bidding the others goodbye, Leviel still tries to scrutinise her. The five of them were at the doorsteps with Mrs Z taking a picture while the coaster bus was waiting for Tirzah, Dove, and Sybil. Tirzah's mother was already on board, reading a book.

Talitha held several red paper bags and handed them to the girls, except for Leviel, who mulled over if she offended her. Then caught Sybil's stare, who was grinning at her.

"Thank you!" Tirzah hugged Talitha the moment she received her gift, only for Talitha to shrug her off. The bubbly girl didn't care and opened the bag. She found a baby blue and pink scarf. "Wow! It's so pretty!"

"You made this?" Sybil tore open hers and shook it at Leviel.

"No, I bought them. Sorry, I have no time." Talitha combed her hand through her front hair. *Who would have the time?*

Leviel chuckled, reading Talitha's mind. She, too, had no time to spare. *Well, if she had an inkling.*

The coaster bus beeped, and off they went.

Leviel and Talitha waved at the leaving vehicle.

"Where's mine?"

"Under the Christmas Tree." Talitha's eyes rounded as she gave Leviel a side glance.

"What? I'm an ersatz, but I too love receiving presents. Besides, I felt left off. You didn't have to put it under the tree. We won't be spending Christmas Eve here. I'll check it."

Leviel ran back inside without waiting for Talitha's answer. She squatted before the Christmas tree and found a box wrapped in shiny red paper. She untied the yellow ribbon and tore open the gift. Laid inside was a red mitten. She tried it on and caught Talitha watching her. "Thanks!" Leviel opened her right palm, and a tiny glass globe materialised in her left hand, and she threw it to Talitha, who caught it without looking. "It's for you."

Talitha examined the globe where an orange tadpole swam at the centre.

"It can grow into a giant toad once you break the glass."

"Indeed?" Talitha kept tapping the glass with her fingers.

"Monstrous in an instant. I suggest you keep it and only bring it to the open space when necessary. You can't hide it then." Leviel returned the mitten to the box. "The angelic houses all get to celebrate Christmas in their respective towers. I couldn't tell you earlier while they were here."

A chime sounded.

"It's here, right on time!" She ran out the door to their mailbox, resembling a miniature house with a cherub sitting atop the roof. Leviel has to poke the cherub's cheek for the flap to open. Inside was a red and gold envelope.

Back at the manor, she handed Talitha the golden envelope. She didn't have to check if it had the House of Shiphrah's crest. Michael's house takes precedence, so they get to use the gold colour. However, Raphaelle would often use yellow but not on official letters.

"This is exciting. How is it different from the gala?"

Talitha attended the recital Thanatos hosted during their second week.

"For one, cherubs will be in attendance. Too many to count." Talitha's jaw dropped. Leviel laughed at seeing her reaction. "Another is the head of your house. He'll drop by."

"Shiphrael?" Talitha asked, who felt a pang in her chest. She didn't even know if a specific archangel existed.

"Michael."

Talitha's eyes turned purple for a moment before they died. Leviel supposed she shouldn't mention the heavenly commander again. So she dragged the shocked Talitha to the icy weather, hoping it would wake her up. They ended up checking the racks of a nearby mall. At a different time, she would find it funny to be shopping with her.

Oh, how mundane her life has turned!

"I'm curious. Why does the mall's furnishing fit the future rather than now?" Talitha asked, sliding her hands over the hangers at a rack they passed by.

"The clock turns whenever some archangels find it suitable to do so. But Galen will remain wherever year it stops."

Leviel held that this place would remain regardless of the mortal world crumbling. So unlike the vision, Raguelle showed her, which made it more disturbing.

"It means this was how it was. Say, in 2024?" Talitha probed further.

"2024?" Leviel frowned. What? Had she lived till then? It wasn't the same year Brianna died. "I wouldn't know. Galen remained unchanged. But the rest of us, mortals and nonmortals alike, also turned with time."

But you and I always go forward, said the white lady. She spoke in her mind out of the blue.

Unfortunately, Leviel replied while her hands fisted.

Was this Absolute Trench's second life? Odd.

They strolled further into the mall, checking the racks of most outlets. An hour passed by before Leviel felt Talitha tugging her arm. Thinking she found a fabulous frock, she halted and gave Talitha a questioning look.

The mortal turned sheepish. "Who can change time?"

Leviel's mouth widened as Talitha's curiosity confirmed her hunched.

What happened when she died as Absolute Trench?

Leviel could not ponder further, for Talitha still waited for an answer. She cleared her throat and masked her thoughts. "Whoever wields the scythe. But I think Michael too. However, you must take my word with a grain of salt. I haven't found a document to support that." Though a pair of midnight blue eyes made her believe he could.

"Death?" Talitha asked, spacing off as she stared at a dress.

Which one? Leviel wanted to assess if she'd figure out there were two. But Talitha nodded and shook her head.

Leviel took two dresses off the rack. "He's not the only one who could wield the scythe. I'll check how these gowns fit." She glanced at Talitha at length and figured she was still calculating the clock's turning. "It's Christmas eve tomorrow. We should talk about something cheery."

Several minutes later, Leviel went out of the fitting room wearing a velvety green V-neck sheer evening gown. She twirled, and Talitha laughed while giving her a thumbs up.

Stunning, heartbreaker, said the white lady.

Well, I take your word for it. Leviel saw Talitha holding the train of a dress on a mannequin. It was a silver beaded spaghetti-strapped chiffon dress. "You want that?"

Ghastly said the white lady. *If she wants it, I'll light it on fire.*

"Not if I wished not to freeze."

Talitha's answer made Leviel relieved. *Well, at least she has a sense of fashion, no?*

The white lady sneered.

Talitha pulled a frock from the rack before giving Leviel a side glance. "Do we have a chariot?"

Leviel's mouth opened as she stared at her. *You can teleport—can't you, Shiphrael?*

I'm a ghost.

You just said you'll light the dress on fire—surely you can bring yourself to the party.

Who said I wanted to visit Michael's abode?

Touché. Leviel's lashes fluttered, then scratched her head. "Sorry! I forgot that you're a mortal. Ever since the tree, I cannot imagine you as a mere mortal." She rubbed her forehead, trying to think of a plan. "I'm sure plenty of angels can teleport you to and from."

Perhaps Michael himself would do the honours, Leviel muttered to the white lady. A grunt was her only response.

After dropping their shopping bags at the manor in the afternoon, the two ended up shivering as they lined up in the street outside a beauty parlour. There were only six hair salons within their little town. Because of the occasion, everyone has customers lining up on the road. They chose the less crowded.

"We should have done this before the mall," said Talitha, frowning.

"Yeah, too late."

Leviel appeared preoccupied, playing snake on her mobile phone—courtesy of Foniel, who does not know she can eavesdrop on anyone.

It was, however, one way. If an angel refused to hear her, she could not very well give them her message via telepathy. She looked up with eyes sparkling as an idea appeared.

"Shall we call Eduard? That stylist last time, where'd he got them?"

Eduard sent an entourage of beauticians to Talitha before Thanatos' gala.

Talitha darted her eyes, appearing hesitant to go that route.

"It's by appointment only."

"It doesn't hurt to ask."

Leviel handed her the mobile phone, where it displayed Eduard's number. Talitha took a minute or two before she accepted it. Several rings went by, but no answer. She rang for the third time before giving up and sent him a text message, then returned the phone.

Midael! Leviel spoke in her head. *Shiphrael needs a helping hand.*

A couple of patrons getting out of the salon with different hairstyles diverted their focus, making them forget the shivering cold.

"Do you think I look better if I cut my hair just below my ears? A new look. It will be on time for New Year's eve. Easier to dry." Talitha appeared to be talking more to herself than Leviel.

"Talitha!"

A girl's voice in the building's corner came. She was in a red Galen oversized hoody, marched to them and handed Talitha two coffee cups. It has a logo from the gentlemen's café reserved for the student council.

"I didn't order this."

"The gentleman over there did." She pointed at a man wearing a pea coat over his suit.

You rang? said Eduard to Leviel while Talitha gave him a frosty look.

"A text reply would have been sufficient." Talitha turned to the girl, accepted the coffee, and thanked her for her service.

She has a point, said Leviel to him.

"What's the use of it when you can do it in person?"

"Hmm." *I'm shutting up.*

Leviel accepted the cup with her name and took a sip before giving him a word of thanks.

"You're welcome," Eduard reached Talitha's side now. It was more for Talitha's benefit, who didn't bother to give him some credit for the drink. "They promised they'll be at your doorstep in another hour," referring to the head dresser. "I see no reason for you to freeze while you wait."

Talitha's frown disappeared. She smiled and batted her lashes at him.

Eduard shook his head. "Whatever it is, the answer is no. I won't be here."

"Oh, why?" asked Talitha

Why? Where's the fire? Leviel seconded.

Eduard near chuckled at their chorus. "I have some duties to attend to."

Such as? Leviel couldn't help but probe further. She didn't mean to pry. It was just how she was.

You sound like a wife, said Eduard and grinned.

Leviel choked on her drink. *Familiar, eh? Did you have one?*

We're treading off course. Besides, it's better that you do not involve yourself.

Ah! Legionary business, she presumed.

Indeed.

Leviel smiled while sipping her coffee.

She thought there was nothing like an emergency to ruin a holiday.

Eduard smirked before glancing at his watch, nodded at her, and then swung back to Talitha. In the next instant, a force teleported them off, and the three stood outside the manor's open small gate. "I'll head off to the House of Shiphrah to book you a chariot for the evening tomorrow. With that said, take care. A Merry Christmas to you. And to you too, Leviel." *Assuming you celebrate it.*

Leviel nodded back and raised the cup of coffee to him. His actions were too suave and smooth. No wonder the girls liked him so much.

Talitha only smiled at him and nodded. "You do the same. Wherever you'd be tomorrow and Christmas day."

"Don't count on it to be merry. Where I'm heading will be of a sombre occasion."

Bloody, you mean, Leviel could not help adding.

Eduard pursed his lips before he disappeared in a blink of an eye.

"Why are Angels busy during Christmas eve?" Talitha asked with eyes looking like saucers.

"Carolling!" Leviel spoke the first excuse she thought of. Then shook her head. "Maybe he's busy making our spring term exam."

Talitha bobbed and thought it wasn't far from Eduard's personality to work on their exam now.

Both shook their heads, meeting each other's gaze. Their laughter echoed as they stepped into the foyer.

14

Fallen Legionary

At precisely six in the evening, on Christmas eve, Heman arrived at their doorsteps. He looked dashing in his formal suit and flattered them with praises. Eduard wheeled the head of the House of Shiphrah to be Talitha's chariot for the evening, showing them he was still in command.

Who could say no to him? Leviel thought. *Or of Shiphrael?*

Leviel took one glance at her reflection before moving away. She wore the emerald velvety V-neck evening gown from the mall. And courtesy of Eduard's dresser, for whom she took advantage, her silky straight raven hair now had turned golden brown and arranged in an updo and some locks.

After several exchanges of flattery, Heeman took pictures of them before they went off to their respective houses.

Upon arriving at the tower housing the angelic members of Tobit, especially the naughty cupids, her jaw dropped. It was just how Thomas had described it. The number of cherubs there surpassed any houses. They were floating outside, and she could see from the arch windows they were overflowing. Even at the fence, a dozen mischievous cherubs lined up, throwing glittering golden sands at innocent passersby that Leviel knew to avoid now. Anyone who doesn't wish to be a fool in love before this year ends must avoid their lane.

At the gates, Coviel trotted over to her. The other cupids from the infirmary sailed behind him. It only meant Thomas was inside. "Lady Khycen," Coviel paused at her legs and balanced himself, trying not to touch the train of her gown. He raised his head, giving her a clear view of his baby blue eyes. "This is for you." He handed her a candy cane.

"Oh, thank you." Leviel accepted it and then froze. *Is he tricking her again?* Leviel narrowed her eyes. The cupid smiled at her, revealing a dimple on both sides of his cheeks without blinking. "Okay, just this once. I would believe you." So she reached for one of his chubby hands. "Do you think we can find Thomas in this mob?"

He nodded, then pulled her inside, not caring for the tail of cherubs behind him, raining golden dust over him. She learned that the dust wasn't potent for the cupids and cupids alone. That irked her the most, for she was a cupid—the heartbreaker cupid. It was fatal to her. She warned the cherubs to stay far from her as she entered the tower. They knew she never bluffed.

Throngs of cupids, younglings and angels crowded several balconies above while golden dust washed the rags of the gallery. Their wings were a nuisance. With the cherubs' inability to stay put combined with their playful character, a ruckus exploded in a corner or another. Three little ones fell off. Then shot back up before they could hit the ground.

Leviel climbed the main staircase diverging into two on the landing while admiring the giant poinsettia-decorated Christmas tree. Heavy snow rained on it. She wanted to catch them, but Coviel steered her to the next flight of stairs on her right. With her tail of cherubs, she started marching from foyer to foyer to find the ballroom. They passed by several Selkirks who mingled with the purebreds. The little ones noticed them, and some flew to give them their gift of love. The ersatz ran fast, bumping and disrupting the other guests.

Leviel cracked up, and so did Coviel. She hunched down and pinched his cheek. Then caught the open doors of the dance hall.

"We're here." Leviel left the cherub and strode inside.

The first one she spotted inside was Nariel, surrounded by senior members of Tobit. He raised his glass of wine to her, to which Leviel nodded in return.

She did a double-take at the massive number of platinum Christmas balls hanging from the ceiling, the kind you can sit on. It wasn't its sheer size that surprised her, but because it was stringless. If the force that held it there disappears, no doubt it can crack the ground, it'll fall on.

"There you are." Thomas walked behind her, holding a wine glass in each of his hands. He handed one glass to her before looking at Coviel. "So, have you given her the cane?" Coviel nodded. "All right, off you go then."

The little one sailed away with his peers to Nariel, who disappeared as soon as they reached him.

Leviel shook the candy at Thomas' eye level. "What's this? I didn't know that cupids have an interest in sweets."

Before he could answer, a babble of glee drew Leviel to the stage where a never-ending rain of sparkling lights fell while a couple of younglings served as target practice for the cupids, dancing while trying to avoid the arrows shot at them. They weren't using a dummy one, she observed. It was a live arrow. If it hits you, your destiny entwines with whomever the chord is connected. The younglings were ersatz.

"Should they be playing with that?" she gestured to the cupids. It was a small mercy that they still failed to hit the youngling.

"No. I believe the cupids shouldn't. Unruly as ever," Thomas shook his head and paused midway as he dashed to the stage. "Siyaniel stopped that!" The arrows froze mid-air. Then both bows and arrows that the cupids held disappeared. "I'll endeavour to speak with the younglings. There can be no doubt they baited the cherubs. The punishment is severe, you know."

"I know. I was a cherub once and mistook myself for a love cupid. As luck would have it, I was the opposite. It was long before I could receive my bow and arrow. You know it. You were there. I'll send a message to my father to orient the young ersatz." Leviel raised one side of her lips before taking two sips of her wine. "A reminder won't do them harm."

Thomas sighed and shook his head. "Oh, where were we?"

"The candy cane."

"Cherub love sweets too. Our creator made the mortals in his image. No child would say no to sweets. Even if they came from fire." He gestured to the cherubs who were now licking it or had a candy cane plugged in their mouth. "I believed the cherubs wanted to cheer their ersatz peer by gifting that cane. That and you need to plaster a smile on your face, Leviel."

She still eyed the candy with suspicion.

"Lightened up."

Leviel plastered a smile and drank her wine. She wished she could. "By the by, does Raphaelle know I'm knee-deep on the web?"

What did I say about lightening up? Thomas muttered on Leviel's head. "She might not know the entire picture, but she has some idea."

"Worse comes to worst even she couldn't stop them."

"Take them in stride. Maybe you won't have to take everything on your shoulders in time."

"You?" Leviel's eyes squinted.

Thomas grinned.

Leviel.

A voice in her head appeared before she could clarify what Thomas meant. She wanted to ignore it, but since he didn't ignore her calling yesterday, she needed to offset the slate. With a dark face, she finished her wine and laid the glass at the side table near them.

"Is there something wrong?" Thomas checked her from head to foot.

"I have to leave."

"You can't. Raphaelle wants to speak to you in private." He shook his head while eyeing the hourglass.

"I'll be right back on time." Leviel activated the doppelt without a contest.

Come, the voice called again. A force teleported Leviel to a garden with green hedges. At the centre sat the life-size statue of tears in heaven. Only the warrior was missing.

Leviel remembered Tirzah and Talitha went here before to complete some cupid's fall ritual. Of course, it didn't end well when Tirzah marked Ezri instead. As the heartbreaker, it wasn't a big deal. Besides, she'll only accept it to be true when she sees the chord that binds the two lovers.

Her pretence at Professor Singh's cottage was to rile Tirzah. She was hoping she'll give her a clue or two about her oddness.

Leviel scanned the place but could not sight her caller's silhouette.

Where are you?

A swish and slush of blades drew her attention. She followed the noise and saw the missing stony legionary battling a headless knight. Swirls of blue light came from the heavens while thunder rained above them. The two now were in gridlock, heedless to the mighty power cloaking them.

A man in a suit with a clerical collar materialised, separating them. His cold blue eyes spotted her. "Take him—now!" he gestured at another fallen legionary who wore a helmet with half a crest plume.

Legatus.

It then revealed the sword piercing through his shoulders.

Leviel could see the pointed tip gleaming near his scapulae. It may take a while for him to spread his left wing. Then her eyes caught the crest on the sword's pommel. Without thinking, she teleported herself and the injured warrior from the place. In an instant, she found herself in an alley flanked by ginkgo trees with dimmed lanterns. Eduard knelt at the centre, unmoving. The sword vanished while fireflies blanketed him. She teleported before him, afraid he'd disappeared with the tiny creatures. Or Raguelle would come to collect.

When she examined him, he only appeared to be bleeding on his head while the injury on his chest disappeared.

Leviel's brows knitted. She knew whose work it was. Raphaelle's. It proves history was correct. He was her favourite cherub once upon a time.

"Oh my, you had a wild party. I can see why you needed my help." Only a member of the House of Tobit can heal a legionary. So Leviel laid her hands on his forehead and Midael's wounds gradually healed. "Is this your thing? Rough."

"Dues need to be paid asap. Of course, I am the one to talk. Thanks for coming," he said, giving her a once over. "Sorry for ruining your night."

"Don't worry. I won't ask for a passing grade." She glanced down and saw a punctured hole in his knees. No wonder he's been kneeling all the while. Leviel hunched down to mend them. "Who was it?"

"It's better that you not know." He darted his eyes to the ground.

"It must be hard for you." Leviel pulled him to his feet and placed his arm over her shoulders. While she dragged Eduard out of the tunnel into the lampless meadow, she saw a lone figure in a dress standing in the woods gazing at the moon.

A witch.

Eduard's weight on her shoulders lightened up, and he now morphed into his suit. A hoot from different directions made her teleport them away. They materialised at a road where beacons of mixed peach and golden glow lit their way. Every place in Galen has a Christmas light powered by electricity. This place was an exemption, it seems. Leviel eyed the angel responsible for it.

"Would it have changed anything? If you had an inkling. And show up there." She pointed to the undisturbed sky, so different from the garden. "Just once. Would it stop him from coming out? Or warn others that something was wrong with him?"

"Thanks for your vote of confidence. I appreciate you not doubting where my loyalties lie." Eduard stared at the lanterns. "Back to your question. I have one in return. What good would it do? We're never to dwell on things we could not change. I beseech you to stop meddling with this, or you'd end up just like Tiyaniel. I didn't call you for a guilt trip, by the way."

"You called me here. I believe you don't call just anyone. You wanted me to see it for myself. It was a brilliant display, but the dead warned me long ago. Why do you think I'm here?"

"Obstinate!" said Eduard, who made her bear more of his weight as they tread the darkened road.

"Maybe, but don't change the subject. A general always knows." Leviel presumed he must've run all over the realms when he had an inkling that something was amiss with his commander. "Why'd you think we exerted efforts to find you after the fall? Rather than search for Samael and Shiphrael? I just didn't realise it was you we were looking for all along."

Remembering just how different he looks wearing his armour from his mortal form.

His purple eyes glowed in the darkness. Shiphrael was a touchy subject.

"What is it you want?" he asked in a whisper.

Leviel didn't answer him until they reached the street leading to the forbidden grounds. The old guard and his squad were absent. "I wasn't just here to help you."

"I figured as much."

Eduard raised his hands, and an electric blue light appeared as several figures in a monk's robe materialised.

Just how much of Michael's forces does Midael have on reserved?

Leviel stood in awe as she witnessed how Michael's right hand summoned several heavenly warriors in a second. Since he was busy, it was time to come out clean.

"I'm here for Azrael's scythe."

Before it could sink into Eduard's mind, Leviel teleported them inside the forbidden ground where a chaos of Galen's army, gargoyles, the old sentinels and some mask creatures fought.

A massive cloud hung above the hidden entrance of the Abyss where Thanatos Galen fought off the assault covered by the fog. It disappeared with a spell from her mouth.

A gigantic golden crown flying fox—the Grigori's army lieutenant revealed itself, making Leviel frown.

She scanned the place, knowing one would never be present without its commander. Eduard had his sword out in the open.

"You'd be my shield tonight," said Leviel, eyeing Thanatos and the fox.

"What—you've gone bonkers."

"I'll only need his scythe for a moment."

Leviel morphed into Tiyaniel's armour before she lunged at Thanatos.

Though surprised, the archangel moved out of her way at lightning speed. She gave chase. Right before she reached him, he disappeared. Thanatos had no time to care for her and let his scythe release explosive energy. It was a while before he realised his scythe was heavier than usual. "Show!" he said, exposing the knight.

With his free hand, he reached over to Leviel, but Eduard in his armour kicked him, throwing him a couple of feet, making Thanatos remove his hold over his scythe. In a blink, a blue stone formed on Leviel's gauntlet, bursting into a wide range of waves. The chaos stopped. Even the Grigoris paused.

Eduard stared at Thanatos with hatred, "What do you mean by this?"

"It's not what you think," he said and morphed into his red robe, becoming more of the real Azrael. With a wave of his hands, Leviel, too, changed into herself. They stared at each other.

"You chased after the Khycen because of the chest. Now you took Shiphrael's life force from Aliya."

Eduard thumped Azrael's chest before pulling at the lapels of his robes.

"It was to stop the immortals from getting stronger," Azrael unclamped Eduard's hands from him. Then jerked his head back to Leviel.

Eduard grabbed Azrael.

"Yet you never surrendered it."

The next instant, a foot kicked Leviel's hands holding the stone. But Leviel vanished before it could touch her.

She reappeared and hid behind Eduard, who glanced at her. Then to Thanatos, who had his scythe form a shield entrapping the woman, who wore a golden mask decorated with serpents. It was then she realised they left the Abyss' entrance unguarded.

Chamuel materialised behind the masked woman.

It wasn't Leviel's scene, and she wanted to leave, but the woman's purple eyes made her stop dead in her tracks. It's her. The woman from the maze. The one who asked her to cut her cord that connected with Chamuel. And like reading her mind, Chamuel noticed her interest in the masked woman, stepped forward and blocked her view.

"Leave," said Chamuel.

"Go!" Thanatos seconded, making Leviel drop her jaw for a moment.

"Happy too."

Leviel bobbed. She teleported to the gates and saw Milo bleeding with three of his peers. Leviel morphed back to her formal dress from the party. "Allow me." She mended their wounds with the wave of her hand.

"Thank you," said Milo, who looked at the sparkling dust on her body. "You're a cupid?"

Leviel looked down at her chest and arms and saw the love powder. She winced, remembering her original form. Without preamble, she teleported back to her original body, deactivating the doppelt mode. As soon as she regained consciousness, she was almost naked in a cubicle decorated with mirrors. Dizziness assailed her, and she saw tiny lit bulbs rooted on the floor while disco music blasted in her ears. Her body felt heavy, pressed into the wall by a male licking her neck. What's more disconcerting is that she can't will her hand to move.

A force grabbed her from him, and she sagged.

Leviel heard a thud, and the naked male fell, letting her see his face. It was Nathan.

15
Heartbreaker's Fall

$\mathcal{B}$eing the overall Commander of the Sentinels, the House of Israfil adopted Haniel, despite remaining a respected member of the House of Mikhail. Over the years, he had paid homage to Raphaelle on Christmas eve. There was no Leviel then. But not this time. He didn't want to risk bumping into her. Not that he didn't wish to. The new year was a week away. It was just too early for whatever fireworks they might set off.

Mikhail's was his choice for the night of cheer then. So there he was, enjoying several jeers and banterings from the younglings. Their talks were about the arrow no one managed to extract besides Talitha. But like the members of Mikhail, he wanted to break Heeman's cockiness.

"Come on. I wasn't there."

"Even Eduard wasn't able to do it. He is Midael, after all!"

"Midael's old," said Haniel, goading Heeman.

Of course, since Midael was their former commander, no one agreed with him.

Heeman was about to say his retort when the lights died. Soon, heavenly cherubs sailed to the stage, lighting the ballroom. It meant Michael drew near. A sound of distant rumble and tintinnabulation of church bells confirmed it. Their merriment halted as they all stood at attention, divided into two groups.

After Michael's brief visit, their clamour resumed. But his cherubs remained, sparring with the others their size. Without their quick reflexes, a dozen would've gone to the infirmary. Still, no one bothered to confiscate their deadly weapons.

The party was in full swing, and Haniel was busy exchanging insults with several legionaries when his lieutenant arrived, informing him of a breach. He scanned the room, watching the rest carrying on with their blissful chats as he listened to the whole gen. By the looks of it, none of them knew of the matter. The first thing that crossed his mind was Lady Khycen. His instincts made him teleport to the House of Tobit. Only to find her well and shooting daggers at Thomas.

Relieved, he exited the tower just when two hammer jeeps stopped. Theodore got out, gave him a salute, and opened the door. "The girl—second year that went missing, I'm afraid, was a witch's doing."

"Which one?" Haniel observed the snow falling in his dinner jacket.

"An elder."

He gazed at Theodore for a while before grinning from ear to ear. "Merry Christmas." Then off fireworks lit the inky sky. When he heard Theodore's answer, Haniel knew it was all the cheer he'd get for Christmas. He stepped into the vehicle without glancing at the colourful explosion. "Search their houses. With the majority gone, it's the best time."

The soldiers who stood at attention followed his orders. Theodore hurried to close the door. Then rounded to the driver's side and climbed inside the jeep. "We need the warrant to enter the council's village."

"Lucky you. We wouldn't need it if we can convince the Mikhails to join."

"Aren't you one?" Theodore gave him a side glance.

Haniel only glared at him.

A few minutes later, they neared the Tower of Mikhail's entrance. Heeman darted from left to right, appearing to cross the street, but paused at seeing them. The jeep stopped just a few paces away from him.

Haniel lowered the window on his side. "With your ability, can you drag Micah here? We need to visit some of his friends," referring to Mikhail's steward and his age.

Heeman smirked while he shook his head. "Not as strong as Talitha."

Haniel took it as his denial and wanted to tease Heeman when a sentinel materialised beside him. It was his scout. He reported that the attack at the Forbidden grounds escalated, and Midael was at the centre. Haniel needed to dispatch his sentinels straightaway to the fight, sending his operation trespassing down the drain. It wouldn't bode well if he left the Galen army unsupervised. He suspects they weren't dealing with a witch they could kill by a bullet.

Dierdre, Sirona and Miriam—are the mighty three. They were on top of his list to interrogate. If he has to guess, his money was on Dierdre. Her obsession with youth and beauty was not a secret.

Just as he stepped out of the vehicle to gather his men, he received a message via telepathy. It was a monster's sighting.

Somehow, Haniel felt like someone was making him run around Galen, stopping him from steering his men in the right direction.

After their tedious search, the soldiers found no clue left by the monster. But since they could not pinpoint the direction it went at random, he'll have to postpone it until daylight comes.

It was near two in the morning when they wrapped it up. So, Haniel brought the men to the SCHQ—the Gentlemen's club. Upon entering, he sensed an immortal's presence. He reckoned too powerful to be one. If he weren't a sentinel, he would miss him. Immortals weren't supposed to stay at Galen during the winter break.

Haniel honed his eyes on them as he paused at the entryway. Dressed in black and ties, they reminded him of vampires—they were in all sense except the biting part. Haniel moved when they entered the back room. He waved to the barista to stop her from greeting him and bumping into Zeus as he did so. The latter slid to the side, avoiding him. The Galen army commander approached the counter and lined up with the others.

Haniel now has his answer why he was busy commandeering Zeus' men.

It was nice seeing you here.

Zeus glanced at him. *I didn't see you.*

Haniel's jaw dropped.

"Talitha from the House of Shiphrah, right?" Haniel heard one immortal ask, making him turn his focus away from Zeus. "Your mates with Leviel from the House of Israfil?"

"Tobit," Talitha corrected.

"Her bacchanalian episodes at Putus will be in the headline after the break. And perhaps even worse if you don't pick her up now."

Find Leviel! Haniel spoke to his sentinels via telepathy. *She's the priority.*

Theodore may only be human, but he sensed Haniel's agitation and turned to him at once.

Haniel twirled his pointer finger.

Theodore bobbed.

With another student army, they rounded the back entrance.

Haniel's chest tightened while his stomach churned. He felt like a puppet and fought his instincts—the string pulling him. A higher being was the only culprit. But there was none nearby he could detect, like earlier. So he remained standing at the entrance.

"Putus?" asked Talitha.

"It's one of ours."

Another member of the immortals chuckled. "He meant our kind's bar. It's in the next town south of here."

Bloody hell! How did we miss that club? Theodore muttered in his head, but Haniel heard him.

"Thanks!"

Talitha dashed out and reached Zeus, who was still waiting for his turn. "I need you to drive me to Putus if you still could. Or you could help me convince one of these angels—" she pointed at Haniel and his men, "—to teleport me there and back."

Haniel strode closer to them.

"Good! There's one." Talitha grabbed Zeus, not caring if he stumbled a bit as she dragged him to Haniel's side, almost slamming him headfirst.

Haniel took a step back as soon as she approached. "Something I could help?"

"There is!" Talitha beamed, while Zeus frowned at Haniel.

Indeed? Were you not eavesdropping?

Mortal. She is mortal for now.

As you know, Zeus paused, then said, "The lady needs you to teleport her to Putus."

"Putus?" asked Haniel, who blinked.

You're playing your role too well, mate.

Are we? Mates?

Talitha darted her eyes from Haniel to Zeus. "I need to pick up a friend."

I suggest you don't waste your time, sentinel. Haniel wasn't familiar with the voice in his head. Since it wasn't Zeus, he looked over his shoulder. A guy with sunglasses who looked paler than a bond paper strode out.

It was a woman Haniel heard, so it wasn't him.

"Hold on," said Haniel and walked over to the immortal. "Sorry mate, my men would've got to delay you." Theodore and the soldier barged in as soon as his words fell. They surrounded the two immortals and escorted them to his vehicle.

Haniel walked back to Talitha, and the scene changed to a darkened room with laser blue and green lights dancing above in tandem with the blasting disco music.

As the Commander of the Sentinels, his teleportation is smoother than any angels. He can bring a room full of people without him lifting a finger.

Talitha and Zeus, caught unprepared, glanced around. Large fluorescent tube-like cubicles flashed at the sides while nude figures swayed in tune with the beat. Talitha dashed to them and found Leviel, with only a pair of her underwear, dancing with Nathan.

She grabbed Leviel, who didn't resist and fell from the steps. Leviel remained on the ground, unmoving. Talitha didn't think she used too much force to cause her to fall. She hunched and examined Leviel's state, whose eyes looked glassy and snapped closed after a few seconds. She appeared to be out of it.

Talitha forced open Leviel's eyelids, revealing a beaded iris resembling those of the dead.

"Haniel! Someone had hypnotised her. If you please, check on the mortal."

Haniel grabbed Nathan, who fell off the floor and didn't get up. It was like Leviel's fall. Zeus turned him over while Haniel checked his pulse.

"He's under a spell."

Zeus walked to the other tubes while Haniel removed his coat to cover Leviel, whose eyes opened. At finding him towering over her, panic assailed her. She turned to her side, saw Nathan, and swung away, spooning herself before hugging her arms.

"Leviel!" Talitha nudged her, but she appeared to have heard nothing.

Haniel touched Leviel's arms, but his powers weren't working on her.

"How could anyone drug and ersatz? And a Khycen at that?"

Talitha knew the hierarchy of Michael's army from Stratagem 101 and where Leviel's family stood.

"Unless she's not on her body."

Haniel recalled the alarm they'd received in the middle of the party. They cannot hide the attack on the forbidden ground from the House of Tobit. Coupled with finding Leviel relaxed and chatting with Thomas, something wasn't quite right then. He should have known better.

It never is if you're dealing with a higher being. It was the same voice at the Gentleman's club.

Out of the blue, several sentinels materialised from above, sending patrons scattering and scrambling to the exit.

"CLOSE THE PLACE!" Haniel placed one arm on Leviel's back and one beneath her legs and carried her. "I'll bring them over to the House of Israfil. You and Zeus wait here. I'll have Heeman escort you."

Talitha nodded, and Zeus appeared beside her.

Ensured of her safety, Haniel disappeared with Leviel in his arms and Nathan in tow.

Upon reaching the tower of Israfil, Haniel paused at the entrance. He whistled. His horse should be able to find Heeman. Between Michael and any cadre, he trusts Michael not to play this kind of game. Especially to a member of his own house. Hence, he needed a Mikhail right now.

As soon as he entered, Thomas was already in the foyer, as if he expected them. He took Leviel from his arms. Then motioned the younglings to take Nathan.

"How'd she end up with a mortal?" Thomas asked, following the angels, who dragged Nathan upstairs. "Where've you been?"

"Sorry?" Haniel's brows knitted. "I've got no recollection my task was to guard her. Where were you?"

Thomas cleared his throat and carried Leviel upstairs while he followed behind him.

Not long after, Heeman appeared, walking alongside Haniel. "Stat?"

"Zeus' men are taking care of the club," Heeman faced front, looking at Thomas' back. "I assume since a mortal is involved, Mikhail can't interfere."

"It depends on whose interpretation."

When they entered the room, they saw Thomas laying Leviel on the bed, who tried to fix herself but only removed the coat covering her, exposing her upper chest. Thomas placed a blanket over her. Without warning, she shuddered and moaned, gripping the blankets. Leviel covered her mouth to muffle the sounds. Too late, it already roused the angels' desire.

Heeman averted his eyes from the bed to Haniel, who was red all over. He'd never seen him so flustered.

Haniel could feel his blood rising to his head while his middle hardened. He closed his eyes, trying to shut Leviel's noise and erased the images it evoked. But the tent beneath his pants remained.

Thomas took Leviel's pulse, touched her head, and removed his hands. He faced the two angels. "The good news is she's untouched. However, whoever slipped her the drug—"

"Was from the House of Tobit or Israfil." Heeman nodded at Haniel, who raised his brows and darted his eyes to Thomas.

"Why would you think so?"

"I've confirmed it. Leviel came out escorted by an angel from the House of Tobit. He might be someone you know."

"Why would someone..." Thomas paused. "Heartbreaker— áthas rúnda!"

Both Heeman and Haniel frowned.

"It's an aphrodisiac."

The two stared blankly at him.

"Potent and deadly to an ersatz. Leviel must mate with her partner—her destined lover. That is the cure."

"What! We're not MORTALS. We do not succumb to such a state!" Haniel grabbed Thomas by his shirt.

Another moan came from Leviel, who seconded Thomas. She clamped her mouth again. Haniel, whose keen sense of hearing was better than any sentinel, cursed inside. His ears burned, and he winced as he let go of Thomas. He appeared to be far worse than them. Then a thought crossed his mind. "Nathan?" His heart clenched at the mention of the mortal.

"Drugged as well. Too frail to have been the culprit," said Heeman, enjoying his discomfort. Thomas cleared his throat to steer them to the matter on hand. Heeman stepped back. "Why don't we send her back to her parents? Perhaps her mother—"

"You want Aluel and Camdiel to see her in this condition?" Haniel jerked his head to him.

"Better than us witnessing her asking for pleasure."

Thomas interjected between them, "No. The poison will peak by then. There is no turning back. She would go insane."

"THEN PRAY WHO CAN FIND HER PARTNER?" Haniel asked, feeling more irritated at Thomas.

"Well, you're in luck." Three cupids materialised on Leviel's bed. "The arrow can be stuck to either of you. Now, which one of you will be her mate?" They looked at Thomas and thought he had grown horns. "Don't look at me like that. Since you're still both here, I assumed you're willing?"

***

Leviel's moans echoed into the faintly lit room while a lone figure stood at the side of the bed, gazing at her face as she reached the height of passion, hurting and unsatisfied in the end. Fisting his hands at his side, Haniel looked heavenward.

When Thomas' words fell earlier, a cupid's arrow struck the core of his heart without his say-so. A series of expletives appeared in his mind that he never dared utter. For so long, he wished they could bury their past. But fate has other plans. It always left him with choices he couldn't accept but must acquiesce to.

Haniel stretched to touch her burning face but retracted it. He closed his eyes, fighting himself. Not that he couldn't do it, his conscience was telling him no. He would be the biggest hypocrite if he did it without her consent. Though, under these circumstances, it still is. He believes that since it was him, with no alternative, even if she consented, it was coercion.

Haniel unbuttoned his shirt with his eyes fixed on her writhing body. He lowered himself to the bed and covered her. In reflex, he closed his eyes as if he savoured his surrender. Then, with a mind of its own, his hands reached her face and caressed her cheeks, feeling their smoothness. She rocked beneath him, and he kissed her forehead, letting the waved passed before holding her face in both hands.

"Leviel," he looked deep into her eyes. "Leviel!" Scared and confused, twin silver saucers stared back at him. "You've been poisoned."

Leviel turned her face away.

"No," Haniel stilled her head. "Listen, I'm Haniel. The Haniel, you hate the most. I am the cure."

Another episode began, and she wiggled beneath him, tormenting them both. Haniel clamped his hands on her arms as Leviel wrapped hers around him.

"Nod off if you understand."

Leviel shook her head.

"Licorice-sweet sometimes called—áthas rúnda."

Leviel's eyes widened, gripping Haniel's sides. *The candy cane.* It crossed her mind for a moment before heat consumed her.

"What?" Haniel glimpsed at her lips, then into her eyes.

"Raphaelle. She—It's her."

Tears slid from Leviel's eyes as the waves of an unsatiated ache heightened.

Haniel lowered his head and licked the corner of her eyes, tasting them. Leviel drew him closer, but Haniel's grip on her tightened, not letting her pull him more. He let what he said sink in first, letting her suffer a couple of waves before lowering his lips to her ears. "There's no escape. But I'll let you choose. We both know Tiyaniel's death wasn't my only transgression to you."

Leviel burst out crying. There wasn't logic in love. *How can their fate be so cruel?*

Haniel moved away, but her hands clutched his arms, digging her nails enough for blood to come out.

"Do you consent?"

Leviel raised her hand and watched the gold and red chord linking them. But the arrow lodged in Haniel's chest still doesn't have its tip. She used her remaining energy to summon the golden scissor to cut the cord.

A millennium ago, Leviel did it right after he stabbed her. She is far worse before than now. She should be able to do it.

Haniel glanced at her arms, also waiting for it to appear. Since Shiphrael was bound to rise, he knew this was the end of Leviel's life. She will never be reborn again. Haniel lowered himself to her and kissed the tears. "If you do it now, there won't ever be you and me."

Leviel nodded.

Haniel kissed her lips and waited until she tugged her mouth open before he darted his tongue in, exploring her mouth and then sucking her lips. Leviel's arms encircled his neck as Haniel pulled the blankets off her and let his roaming hands take free rein on her body.

He tugged one breast, and Leviel's moans echoed again while his body ignited. His lips slid down to her neck, onto her chest, only to find her body covered in chartreuse lights before she vanished.

When he turned to his right, he found a silver-haired, chubby older woman, near four feet tall with hazel-green eyes, holding a wooded staff twice her size beside the bed. "You're the cure?" asked Sirona.

Haniel stood abruptly, only for Sirona to swing her stuff, striking his head. He fell off the bed. She nudged his body, and at finding it lifeless, she threw saliva on his face. "Degenerate!"

Sirona vanished a few seconds later while cupids and angels barged into the room. "Where's the witch?" Heeman asked, then paused at finding the bed empty. "Where's Leviel?"

"A witch trespassed on Israfil?" Thomas marched to the bed and found the knockout Haniel surrounded by the others. He cleared his throat. "Out! Not a word!"

When only he and Heeman remained, Thomas placed a vial beneath Haniel's nose, and he awoke.

Haniel rubbed his head and wiped his face with his shirt.

Heeman grinned and whistled. "You can only catch a sentinel off guard when he is on top of—"

Haniel threw a pillow on his face before he could finish his sentence.

"I meant preoccupied," Heeman hid behind Thomas.

"Right, so did you cure her before Sirona appeared?"

Haniel's face darkened as he eyed Thomas. "The candy cane. I take it, your cherub."

Thomas averted his eyes and sat on the bed. "Reporting this to her grace as a failure would be a headache."

"I wish it'll hurt as much as my head now."

"But not as much as seeing Leviel's pained eyes." Thomas rubbed his head. If she'll ever speak to him again, he thought.

"Indeed." Haniel wore his coat, now dressed and dapper. "I am curious, however. Why go to all these troubles?"

"A wager and a quota."

"BET? I feel insulted."

"Raphaelle needed your love to prove she can make a miracle. Love overcomes hate." Thomas twined his arms and shook his head. "The bet is between her grace and the father. Well, with Uriel's urgings. The quota, should she prove love, is the answer, could stop this mess involving doomsday."

Haniel and Heeman cracked up. When Thomas didn't join in, their laughter died.

"Are you serious?" Heeman loosened his bow ties.

"When was I ever not?"

"Just how many points are they worth? Ten mortals? A hundred?"

Thomas still shook his head. Heeman presumed he didn't know it himself.

"Raphaelle has too much time."

Haniel eyed him to stop him from saying more.

"All right!" Heeman raised both hands, backing off. But he needed his point sent across. "It's not possible if we based the history of the fall."

"Agree. Raphaelle should place her faith more on Shiphrael. She has better chances of letting bygones be bygones than having Leviel and me get on with love. At this rate, hell will freeze before we can bed without Sirona's interference. I doubt I'll ever forget her."

This time, Thomas joined in with Heeman, laughing at the image Haniel painted.

He gave the two a hard stare before he bobbed and vanished. After a minute, he materialised at a well-lit beech tree tunnel, feeling disoriented. He didn't mean to be there. Haniel shook off the throbbing pain in his head.

A figure came out from the shadows.

"Late night?"

Haniel blinked. His voice was like his, and he appeared exactly like the face he hid. The figure smirked before covering his face with a silver mask. "Don't worry. I'll be quick."

16

The End

Leviel was in Sirona's arms when they appeared at an empty road beside a clear turquoise river. A brilliant contrast to the snow cloak scenery of Galen. It only meant they were near the dragon's gate—a rare portal leading to the nixie world. As far as Leviel knew, except for heavenly angels, none can teleport to Galen. Hence, for emergencies, the gate was necessary. But it doesn't mean anyone can just pass.

"Why is it open? I don't recall I allowed it," said Leviel to Sirona as she laid her at the foot of the willow tree.

"Because you did not." Sirona placed her hands on Leviel's forehead, and chartreuse light engulfed her. The pain from the poison subsided, allowing her to breathe without biting her lips, albeit momentarily. For it to be permanent, she needed the cure. A wind chime rang not far before an emerald light materialised and split.

Two older women shorter than Sirona appeared.

Leviel reckoned they were the two powerful witches—Sirona had a close bond. Her eyes fixed on the dishevelled elderly lady with a burned arm. She knew of those purple burns from her dreams. It was from Shiphrael's fire and twice as excruciating as the poison.

Leviel admired her endurance and assumed she could only be Miriam. The other must be Diedre.

Sirona ran to the injured witch and tried to cure her, forgetting that she'd used much in Leviel earlier. "Sorry. I forgot that if she couldn't heal herself, there wasn't much use for my powers, either.

Miriam nodded and strode to Leviel's side, whose entire body shook as another wave of pain passed.

Could a heartbreaker not escape cupid's painful matching? The world turned upside down.

Miriam's thoughts were clear to Leviel, who looked away from her, not wanting to see her pitiful gaze. Then she jerked her head back right when Miriam hunched as she touched her forehead. There was something familiar about the witch, as if they'd met. An odd feeling that they were friends.

"Will you be able to undo the poison?" Sirona asked as she wiped the sweats on Leviel's forehead.

"I could put her under a spell to fall for someone else. Only the archangel who made the poison could heal her."

"I can assure you it's not on her agenda." Leviel gritted her teeth as her heart burned with anger more than the pain.

Miriam's right palm now had a salmon day glow, and she shrugged. "The poisoned will wane in a day. Let's give it a go, eh?"

Both Leviel and Sirona shook their heads.

"No."

"She doesn't have much time."

"It's her fate then." Miriam forced her palm on the heartbreaker's chest before their protests fell.

Leviel roared, and tears fell from her eyes while her vision doubled. The arrow lodged in her chest more profoundly than before, bleeding her.

"If the poison won't kill her, the pain would!" Diedre, watching at the sides all the while, pulled Miriam, and the pain lessened. Sirona didn't care about their squabbles and placed her hands over Leviel, who grabbed her arm.

"No." Leviel knew she intended to use her last ounce of energy to numb her pain. Instead, she summoned herself into a cupid's dominion, easing it to a level that allowed her to think.

Miriam grunted as she felt her burned arm scald more than ever while boils formed in Sirona's face. Dierdre disappeared in a blink.

"The legionaries are getting closer. We must go!"

Miriam pulled Sirona to her feet.

"I can't just leave her here. She's the last of the Khycens."

"She's Leviel. They would never let her die as long as Shiphrael remains." Miriam waved her hand, and thick soot cloaked Sirona, and she vanished. Miriam tucked an object into Leviel's palm. "Hang on there, heartbreaker."

The cupid's dominion repelled Leviel, and the pain surged back into her system. It was useless for her to decline.

Then a sudden metal thud behind Miriam forced her to disappear at once. Milo materialised in her place. Three more metal steel thumps followed, casting a great wave while earth debris flew to Leviel, but a shield covered her. It was Milo's. Three sentinels and two legionaries surrounded them and scanned the place.

"Chase the Grigori!"

A legionary warrior she'd never met ordered, and they flew away.

At hearing the word Grigori, Leviel's eyes widened, and her heart skipped a beat. Milo approached Leviel, but she shook her head. "Go! Duty first."

He looked at her with sad eyes before he bobbed and vanished before her. Another intense pain struck her, and she writhed, mewled, and bit her lower lip.

A sound a few meters away made her jerk in its direction as if sensing an enemy, and she saw a pair of red deer's shiny ebony eyes peeping at her. Leviel remembered it from the clearing that guided her to the Khycen's old HQ. Then of Tiyaniel's diary. She gazed up and saw the scarlet moon between the willow boughs looming above. Leviel's heartbeat sped, and she glanced back to the deer, only to find it gone.

A blood moon isn't a good sign.

She felt a burning pain in her hand and opened it, revealing a rough fist size cobalt-coloured stone. It was akin to the ones Aliya held. Except it was not just any stone. It was a legionary's sapphire stone that stores their reserve powers. They used it to speed up their recovery.

Why would Miriam have it?

What bothered Leviel the most was why she recalled seeing hundreds of them around a toddler's height clamped on the ground. She probed her mind, but a ringing sound in her ears made her wince and stop. Leviel felt faint again and touched her bleeding heart. At least her painful urges stop.

The strings on her arms thickened while the chord connected to the arrow on her chest thinned. Haniel's life force was waning, and she sensed he was closed to her. Her eyes darted to the darkness and touched the string linking them. It gleamed to the river across, connecting to Haniel's body dangling in the air before a man whose arm extended towards him.

"Haniel!"

Her heart stopped when he turned. Blue veins bulged on his forehead, almost breaking his ashen skin as he fought an invisible hold wringing his neck.

She quivered.

Leviel, I'm sorry.

Haniel burst into tiny dark moths.

"No!" She reached her hands to him and struggled to stand, but the searing pain took hold of her as if it ripped her chest open. It nailed her back to the ground, face down. "Ahh!" Leviel teleported to a sitting position, leaning on the tree while squeezing the stone harder. She was soon out of breath, and sweats covered her. When Leviel spun to her side, she saw the culprit across the river gazing at her. She felt as if a cold bucket of water had dropped on her head.

The man walked to the banks and removed his mask. Leviel choked and quieted while she shook her head. *No! It can't be you.*

Why can't it be me?

In the next instant, he teleported before her. Only to fly back five paces away, avoiding a scythe that struck the ground.

A red hooded figure materialised before Leviel while a blast of wind passed. Death extended his hand, and the scythe flew back to him.

Why is he here? Leviel glared at Thanatos. *Is he here because of Shiphrael's life force?*

"The monster everyone is looking for, eh? I thought my reaper had too much to drink."

"You sought the chest. Yet you didn't even realise my existence," said Haniel, who put on the silver mask. The lamp post dimmed until the light disappeared. But it burst into a blinding light, stopping his escape. When Leviel blinked, he saw Thanatos' silver scythe hit Haniel, who flew into a tree. Before the scythe could slash him, a flaming light materialised, morphing into a seven-year-old child.

Raguelle took the blow and returned it.

"Pardon me," said Thanatos to Leviel.

With lightning speed, she found herself in his arms in the air, avoiding the eruption in a hair's breadth. *Who would have thought Death would hold her in his arms to save her?* Leviel bet no ersatz would believe it. She's finding it hard, too.

A chartreuse coloured lights swirled in the air, morphing into Sirona. She pointed her staff at them.

Hazel-coloured energy wrapped around Leviel, and she sailed down to her.

Thanatos grabbed her back, undeterred by Sirona's power.

Sirona's staff broke suddenly while red and gold light appeared between them. It materialised into Thomas carrying a young man's body on his shoulder. A thick smoke cloaked Sirona while Thomas dropped the body to the ground and shot a golden lightning bolt at her. The soot cloaked, deflected it.

"Show!" Thomas waved.

The dark smoke morphed into Miriam's figure.

"A Grigori." Before his words could fall, his palm emitted a reddish glow, blasting Miriam across the river, and Thomas went after her.

Sirona ran to the river's edge, but a white golden dragon took her away. "Leviel! I must save her!"

"Go!" said Leviel to the dragon. It flew towards the dragon's gate. She knew they wouldn't have returned if it wasn't for her. But if Thomas gives an order, Leviel can't defy him. He was Raphaelle's second in command. It's better to save her first.

The loud blast across the river made Leviel grip Thanatos' robes, who shook his head. "No. You need the—"

Two inky clouds of smoke hurled past them, and Haniel and Raguelle tailed them over the river to the fight.

A grunt from the ground distracted Leviel. The body Thomas left turned to his front, and Leviel recognised him as Emmet. Then the beggar's grim face appeared in her mind. Beaded sweats grew more on her face. "This isn't happening." Her necklace rose, and the locket opened. Emmet disintegrated into ashes. His remains sailed across the river.

"Interesting," said Thanatos, whose lips now set in a hard line. Within a second, they crossed the river.

The giant reptilian monster battled with Miriam while Thomas and Raguelle contended with two monstrous, apelike bats.

Their steel-like wings took Leviel's notice.

No! It can't be.

They were the same Grigori Lieutenants from the forbidden ground. They always come in pairs. It only meant someone with a higher rank was already inside Galen. A dark smoke made Leviel turn to the other fight. It came from Miriam, who fought the beast. She was holding well despite being wounded. Leviel only hoped she wasn't their commander. If it were her, then it meant death for the entire Selkirks.

The sudden absence of pain in her body made her blink. She touched her chest only to feel a stiff hand. Leviel glanced down and saw Thanatos holding the arrow's tip.

Her brows knitted as she stared at the side of his face while he watched the fight. *I could put her under a spell to fall for someone else.* Miriam's words rang in Leviel's head, making her grip and pull his hand.

"Let go."

Thanatos didn't. "It'll hurt more." Then he turned, and their eyes locked.

No, no. It better not be him.

Blinding light bursts, and their heads swing back to the action.

Zev emerged between Miriam and the monster, upside down with his left palm on the ground, emitting a bright light surrounding them, forming a pentagram. It was the seal of Solomon. The chain around Leviel's necklace broke as it flew towards heavy eddies of wind mixed in with black ashes. It swooped into the formation while a dozen golden moths swirled out from the monster's forehead, joining at the centre. Those within the pentagram froze.

The swirls morphed into a figure covered in a black hooded robe with a staff. Leviel couldn't help but stare at the teal-coloured rock at its tip. She saw the same magical stone nestled in her parent's chamber. When the figure lowered its hood, gleaming silver eyes made eye contact with the monster's, which transformed back into Haniel's form. A hole opened between his browse, emitting an inky beam shooting straight at Miriam's, whose beaded eyes blackened. She changed into a youthful girl. Dark, thick soot burst out from her, and Haniel absorbed them. Zev, who recovered, rushed between them and drew the soot from Haniel. The light from the seal on the ground waned.

Tiyaniel stomped his staff on the ground, increasing the seal's power, halting them mid-air. Then he kicked Zev out of the formation, making him break his hold on Haniel. The smoke transferred to Tiyaniel instead.

"No!"

Leviel jumped from Thanatos' arms into the formation. The seal shot out a liquid light as soon as she entered, barricading them inside it. Paralysed, she watched as her necklace drifted before her while the clock inside burst. White dove feathers rained, and a clock rang inside the seal.

After the fall, ice covered the earth for thousands of years. The archangels retreated to their realms, and the sentinels resumed their post. The ersatzes were new and guarded the mortal realm. However, their existence was on the verge of extinction. And while they fought for survival, heaven sent the sentinels to scour the human world and find the fallen Midael. Raphaelle commands the Khycen clan to assist them.

After receiving a clue from the Khycen scouts, Leviel, young and wilful, gathered a small contingent without Tiyaniel's knowledge. Her instincts tell her it was credible. Eager to be the clan's heroine, Leviel set out. It led them to the frozen lake at the mountain's peak, so far up that a mortal would freeze before reaching it. It was also the place the original Lord Khycen forbade them to roam.

Leviel believed it was why it was a perfect hideout for a legionary.

It was only a seventy-two-hour journey. Along the way, she lost the lives of her men. They either got sick or lost their minds. But she didn't give up. She thought that if she did, their deaths would be in vain.

Leviel arrived at the peak unharmed, but the cold sipped into her bones, making her pause with each step. She stood stunned by the sight of the lake as she peeked through the trees. Hordes of cobalt blue legionary stone sprouted from the lake surrounding a frozen warrior with a black chromatic coloured sword wedged in his chest—the only one unfroze. A distant rumble from an avalanche alarmed her, but she kept walking closer to the lake. When Leviel neared the edge, the stones gleamed, and she felt her body warm. Two giant stones sunk into the water, giving her a clear path to the warrior. The water shook while the ice where Leviel stood slanted, and she skidded to the Legionary. She steadied herself, but her powers were nonexistent. Leviel slid further to the centre. The sound of a horse's hooves came, and Haniel and Tiyaniel appeared. But in a blink, her hands wrapped around the black chrome sword, which emitted electric energy, surging to her arms while it blasted the rocks.

"Stopped!"

"No!"

Panic assailed her, and she willed herself to stop, but her hands won't obey. Leviel pulled it, and she sailed in the air. She could only watch as lightning bolts struck the sword, and her ascent halted.

"At last."

Dark smoke exploded from the Legionary's chest and his midnight blue eyes opened, locking with Leviel's. He burst out from the ice, and the frozen lake cracked before it crashed.

Haniel flew and hugged her from behind while Tiyaniel struck his sword on the stones surrounding the Legionary.

A brilliant light illuminated the lake's surface into Tiyaniel's forehead, where the Seal of Solomon appeared, mirroring those that covered the lake.

"Leviel, let go of the sword! You will kill Haniel!"

She spun to find his veins bulging while his teal-coloured eyes beaded and blackened.

With all her strength, she willed her hand to comply. One of her hands let go and stretched to Tiyaniel, transferring thick ashes to him. His veins thickened, and his eyes beaded like Haniel.

Horrified, Leviel cried and dropped her hand, but a force kept it there.

"Thank you," said the Legionary.

Leviel glanced at his face, then at the engraved golden tree on his breastplate. Midael. Why are you doing this?

"Do I look like I have an oren on my neck?" the Legionary asked, reading her thoughts.

"You're not he. It is I you searched for," came a voice above them before a blue rioting lightning bolt struck the Legionary. The force threw Haniel and Tiyaniel away from Leviel, who remained poised in the air, holding the sword.

A figure in a black monk's robe with purple eyes extended his arms sideward, gathering lightning bolts into his fists.

"You can't destroy what you created that easily." The Legionary stood unharmed and sent Midael a dark rioting blow with equal power. The two soon duelled in the air.

Leviel felt a piercing pain in her left arm. Yellow, green liquid came out from her wounds and into the sword. Its hold loosened, and she came down. "If the monk is Midael. Then who is he?"

"An abominable rock."

Tiyaniel tapped her back, freezing her in place while he took the sword, burning his hands. With all his might, he threw it at Haniel, who swooped into the fight. He caught the sword and stabbed it to the Legionary's back. The Seal of Solomon formation died, and the Legionary and the monk vanished in a blink. Tiyaniel and Haniel fell into the lake that froze in a second.

Leviel broke Tiyaniel's spell and scrambled to save them.

Midael appeared once more and saved them instead. She could not help but stare at the oren on his neck and his baldness. He laid them on the side of the lake. Leviel hurried to them and summoned her powers to heal them. When she held her hands above their chest, dark ash radiated, and she retracted them. Stuck on her palms, akin to a lump, were two red jewelled stones from the dark chrome sword's pommel. Leviel picked the stone using her fingernails, but to no avail. So she pulled the dagger from her side belt, but a beam of emerald light shot out from her forehead. Then her arms turned pale, and her veins bulged. She froze. Midael clamped his hand with hers, absorbing the dark powers within her. A behemoth serpent surrounded by the eternal fire assailed Leviel's thoughts, and she felt her body burn.

"Ahh!"

Tiyaniel broke free from the trance, swung his stuff, and the barricade of light disappeared. A dark swirl of lightning struck him. To his right was Leviel. Dark wings sprouted on her back as she faced Miriam's now youthful look, unlocking her memory.

One thing is clear now why Haniel stabbed her then. The girl whose child the sentinels took was a Grigori. She wasn't just any Grigori. The youthful girl was Samyaja's daughter, which meant she controlled anyone infected with the devil's ice. A sickness they called for the ersatz who trespassed on that mountain and survived. They turned to the Grigori's side. Worst, they grew a pair of dark wings overnight. By order of Heaven, the sentinel sentenced them to death. It's why they were on the brink of extinction.

Leviel glanced behind her and paled.

A body slammed into her, and she felt a stabbing pain in her stomach that made her stumble. Leviel watched as the mask on Haniel's face fell while her arms hugged him. She peeked over Haniel's shoulder. Hunched behind him was a legionary in dark chrome armour—the same headless warrior from the garden yestereve. His hands were on his sword, whose blade still pierced into them. However, he wasn't headless now.

"We can't have you having wings, Heart—"

With her last ounce of strength, she shoved the stone Miriam gave her into his mouth while the strings on her arms connected to the two tips of golden-red arrows lodged in his chest. Leviel pulled them out.

"No!" Bright blue lights exploded from his eyes and mouth before he morphed into his mortal form, dressed in a military fatigue uniform. Zev was beside him at once and covered them with a shield before Thanatos' scythe could strike them. "You're not playing nice."

"And stabbing is?"

Her powers died, and with Haniel's weight, they fell. Blood trickled from Haniel's mouth down to Leviel's neck as tears fell from her eyes.

"Leviel! Haniel!" Tiyaniel ran to them.

As he touched Leviel's hand, a flick came in her ears, and the scenery changed to a familiar empty street flanked by ice-cloaked fields while a blizzard grew thicker over the horizon. The same gate she must enter at her life's end opened to her left. Three statue-looking gatekeepers still waited at the hanging arc walkway. However, the middle angel jumped down and looked behind her.

Leviel spun and saw Haniel poised in the air with his silver mask off and the Legionary's sword wedged in his back. Blood spilt out from his body to the ground. She again felt pain in her stomach where the Legionary's sword stabbed her. Her hands came up and covered her open wound as she fell and spewed blood on the pavement.

"What a pity. Two hearts. Raphaelle, her grace, believed them to be a means to save the fallen from heaven's wrath. Only to disappear in this manner," said one gatekeeper.

The snow grew thicker while her blood mixed in with Haniel's froze on the ground. It made her remember the distant past before the tragedy.

> *Eleven-year-old Leviel peered behind Raphaelle while she introduced Haniel to the clan.*
> *"He would be your mate in the future."*
> *Leviel's eyes widened while her jaw dropped.*
> *The angel smiled at Leviel. Raphaelle laughed as she took his and her hands and placed them together.*

It was a beautiful memory.
With that, the heartbreaker's consciousness ended.

17
Master of Love and Destiny

Before midnight, a pair of legs dangled in the air before it revealed its complete form. It was of a woman dressed in a yellow Grecian-style gown. The sparkling diamond necklace she wore emphasised her sense of importance. One would have thought so. All stone was as big as a baby's fist. The cruise ship sunk a little deeper, with no one noticing, anchored on the shores. Ripples appeared on the surface of the water below when her feet touched the deck, but were not strong enough to rock the ship. If it did, it would be from the mob of youthful patrons' wild dancing party. However, the woman wasn't interested in it.

She went to a bar at the opposite end of the ship. Most customers were matrons in their late forties and early fifties lounging at the readied seats, serenaded by a jazz singer. They wore their best frocks, displaying the jewels they hid and showing off on these occasions. Mellowed and subdued was the overall ambience.

Maybe, she thought. *But their minds indeed weren't.*

If one weren't used to the scenery, one would feel out of place. As soon as a person entered the door, the ladies at the bar weighed their worth. Most owners of these prejudiced eyes weren't from the upper class. There's Mary, whose husband sits high in the ranks of a million-dollar company but on the operational level. However, she loves to brag that he's an executive. There's Rita, whose husband works on a commission basis and had saved a lot so that she could join that cruise. But she painted him as a wealthy husband with enough spare for her vice. Then Georgina, whom everyone thought was still happily married. She received the cruise ticket from her soon-to-be husband after she divorced her current one. And the list went on. Not all were like them. There were also a handful of decent wives on board, but it wasn't her choice of a circle to ingratiate herself. The odd woman prefers the wives of hard-working men. Those whose wants they'll never be able to satisfy.

She watched these not-so-decent matrons scrutinise her from head to toe. Their jeers and smirks on their faces were clear for her to see, despite the dim light. Even better, she could hear their thoughts.

She's here again. Oh, this would be a lovely evening.

She is indeed thick-skinned. She hasn't had enough of our jabbing remarks.

Oh! That diamond. Tonight's set was indeed larger than the rest she'd worn before.

I bet those gems aren't genuine. The ugly woman only has one set of gowns.

I need to squeeze from the woman where she bought the necklace. Mine would fall out soon.

"Hi gals!" she greeted them.

The matrons couldn't help but laugh at her. She wasn't part of their niche. But she was over-friendly with them. It wasn't only because she wanted to enter the group that bothered them or her unknown background; it was her overall aesthetics.

The odd woman grinned, opened her powder mirror and observed her massive dark curly hair, crescent eyes, large lips and a pair of rabbit front teeth resting outside her lower lip. Her thick make-up made her look paler than she was. With only five feet and two inches tall, she compensated for her lack of height by wearing three-inch heeled shoes. But same dress for three nights. One matron had the guts to ask if she had her dress washed.

She, however, didn't approach these matrons tonight and sat far from the bar. A waiter came, and she ordered a bottle of scotch.

"Oh, what's this? A sudden shyness from our group?"

"Awful night?"

"Feeling the season colder than ever?"

"At least she got our point."

"She's just sulking."

"After we ignore her, she'll come running back.

The odd woman was indeed having a disappointing night. It wasn't her first stop for the evening. She first dropped by at a province six hours behind. Only to find her targets weren't present.

Bored, the odd woman scanned the far end of the lounge. Her eyes settled on a young man drinking a beer. He was the typical armour-plated character, with only a pair of jeans and a shirt. The weird glances he got from most patrons went unheeded. Then her eyes admire the open buttons of his shirt, revealing his muscular chest. A shriek from the corner made her drop her gaze.

Good. About time. The odd woman thought. *It's why she came.*

Near the stairs, Mrs Lintz had both her arms pulled by two men. One was her husband, and the other was her lover. These three were the talk of town aside from herself.

"Let go!" Mrs Lintz tugged her arms from them. The men gripped her arms even more. She suspects she'll have bruises tomorrow.

"You let go of her," said Mr Lintz to the young man ten years his junior. If one would compare them based on looks, none could tell one was out of the other's league despite their age disparity.

"No, you let go. You don't love your wife."

"And you do?" Mr Lintz asked, raising his brow.

Mrs Lintz looked more irritated than hurt at their question.

"Do they?" Thomas asked. He appeared suddenly, still garbed in his formal wear. "Of all the faces you could—" He choked in his words, seeing the odd woman's face darkened. She took a sip from her glass and turned her face away from him. Thomas rounded to her other side. "Evening, your grace."

The matrons at the bar who noticed them squealed at seeing him bowing at her.

"Are men blind now?"

"The diamonds are real."

"I think so too."

"Or his drunk as a skunk."

"Go away," said Raphaelle to Thomas, observing his velvety coat. They were six hours behind Galen. It was too warm for his kind of dinner jacket.

"Shall we dance?" He still has his waist bent, waiting for her answer.

She looked at his stretched hand and took one gulp of scotch before clutching the bottle to her arm. It disappeared in an instant.

Thomas shook his head.

"What? It was expensive." Raphaelle stood and reached for Thomas' open palm. "I take it. It didn't go well with your goddaughter."

As the two passed by the bar, the matrons' drinks became warmer. Mary choked on her drink, and Raphaelle stared at Thomas.

"I never took you for someone who thirsts for vengeance." Of course, it was the pot calling the kettle black, she thought. "Leave them. It's Christmas eve."

"I'm here for the cure." Thomas twined his hand with hers, the other on her back, as he pulled her to him.

"Here, I thought you'll let the witches scatter their brains for it."

"We both know they're no match for you."

They swayed with a music beat of their own. Raphaelle's eyes were still at the couple near the stairs. Two of her fingers pointed at them, and the men released Mrs Lintz. *Go with the one you love. If it's yourself, then set them free.*

Mrs Lintz's head swung from left to right. Thomas noticed her eagerness to find the voice in her head.

I am your conscience, he said.

Raphaelle stomped her foot into Thomas, who only winced and endured.

"Mortals could never take a hint! Look at them. None of them had arrows lodged in their hearts. I assume Leviel cut it a long time ago."

Thomas's brows knitted and saw it for what it was. "Then why are they still attached?"

"Desire."

Thomas observed them more. He supposed Mr Lintz desired prestige. He thinks being divorced won't bode well on his résumé. The wife wanted to feel young and adored. And the young man lusted after the woman's money. Then his eyes darted to the several looks at the bar.

"The matrons. Friends of hers?"

"If friendship means to be pretentious—la-di-da, and competitive at every turn. Then yes, I suppose so."

"What has the world become?"

"Bitter. It's a shame. I'm Raphaelle, but I'm naïve. In my arrogance, I thought love was enough. Uriel stimulated me to do research, saying I was out of touch. He was right—and no! You cannot say I said so. By the by, where is he? He seemed to have disappeared since the tree incident."

"Oh, you miss him. Will you allow the cupid to strike—"

A distinctive sound of a chain rolling upwards, deep in the water, caught Raphaelle and Thomas's attention, forgetting his teasing statement. With the blasting music, an ordinary mortal could not detect it. The next instant, the ropes and chains that held the ship to the shore ruptured. Some passengers aboard felt dizzy and swayed. The attendees at the wild party crashed into each other.

"Well, perhaps someday you'll take up that offer. But for now, Galen is in disarray," said Thomas, answering his question. "I didn't give any helping hand earlier when uninvited guests broke in." Then he whirled and flew them further to the observation deck, where they saw three high-ranking Grigoris trying to break the shield near the port. "

"It appears you forgot your tails."

"A hazard with being your right hand. For sure, none knew I was meeting you. Did your study bear any fruit?"

"Desire. Love and hate are nothing compared to it. Both will disappear at the slightest hint that I would fulfil their wants."

"Then are you giving up on your wager?" Thomas asked. He saw the couple still arguing despite the chaos.

"No. Not at all." Raphaelle morphed into her angelic form, open for everyone to see. In the next second, several more pairs of eyes were on them. "You were asking for the cure?"

Thomas nodded as he glanced around, finding one lone man sitting on the floor with his knees between the railing. Taken aback, Thomas inspected him. He didn't notice him before. When the man caught his stares, Thomas pivoted to Raphaelle.

"Meet Emmett."

Raphaelle pointed at his chest. The golden arrow the cupid hit Haniel before didn't have its tip. But Emmett has the same arrow with its end. "The first fragmented soul Tiyaniel experimented on to hide his own."

"He's the cure?"

"No. But Emmett's your priority at the moment." Raphaelle turned as the Grigori soldiers broke the shield and flew to the ship. Then they hit the deck with a loud thud, right when the wild party threw champagne and wished each other a Merry Christmas. Giant splashes rained on the deck, and the ship swayed.

A powerful wave shifted the ship to the left while more water swashed onto the deck. Wrapped in golden light, Thomas rose, spreading his thirty-foot long wings while a dozen golden arrows rained on everyone below. Then he flew away with Emmet on his shoulder.

The soldiers disappeared, then came back. The arrows stuck on the deck turned to ash.

Raphaelle cleared her throat.

A blinding globe of yellow enveloped her. She was wingless, while her large train of yellow frocks floated around her. Their mouths opened.

Bloody hell! Why is she here?

We should have known the shield wasn't Thomas's.

"Hello, soldiers!"

Raphaelle extended her right hand and gestured for them to come.

It made them rage, and they came to her at once. Raphaelle, of course, understood their outburst. She imprisoned their leader, and every one of their kind wanted a piece of her.

All three jumped at the shield, but they froze mid-air before they could touch the orb. In comparison, everyone on the ship stopped moving.

"The great flood wasn't reliable." Raphaelle shook her head at the Grigoris. She brushed past the humans and checked the soldiers one by one. "So was the ice that followed." Then she gazed at the fireworks frozen in the sky. If the mortals now could see Shiphrael's rain of fire, they would appreciate none of this scenery. Then she stopped before the last Grigori soldier. He wasn't a Nephilim. The scar on his left eye confirmed it. She knew how he got it when he was little. Although Raphaelle long lost count of the Grigoris she killed, melancholy could still make her heart bleed. It was unavoidable for her to encounter high-ranking Grigoris, who were once little cherubs raised by her. Such as tonight.

"Can you blame me for following orders?" she asked.

The soldier blinked as if a hint of his innocence remained. Raphaelle laughed, wanting to see anger instead of a pair of beseeching eyes. A lone tear slipped from her eye, while the image of Midael, Shiphrael, and Lucifer as cherubs emerged in her mind. She wants nothing more than to cry for injustice.

"The cure," came Azrael's voice, pulling her from the gloom. Her face cringed. "Come on! She's in the in between."

She waved, and the fireworks disappeared.

"Why is Gabrielle interfering?"

"It wasn't her plan. It was you who handed Leviel."

"If you say so," Raphaelle smirked and fisted her right hand. The Grigoris burst and dissolved into ashes. "Well, since you seem to care, let me give the heartbreaker the cure."

A giant wave stood surrounding the ship while a swirling pool hurled it. "I'm sure tonight's tragedy will make you forget what you saw. And, perhaps, your mind could be kinder to others."

Raphaelle looked at the frightened mortals. Then gestured to the dozens of ersatz who materialised in the air. They all bowed to her. "Make sure everyone survived."

Without waiting for their answer, a blinding red light shrouded her, and she disappeared from the ship. In a blink, Raphaelle appeared just when the giant clock chimed and sucked everything of the in-between. The golden and dark butterflies intertwined as they sailed towards the clock. But time froze when her bare feet touched the ground before the giant clock.

A red light captured the butterflies, pulling them back right before they entered the tunnel. Raphaelle gazed at the red hooded figure beside her, standing as large as the giant clock. Azrael held his golden scythe in his left hand. The gatekeepers stepped away from their bridge, allowing the demons to enter. Azrael spun, and his hood lowered, revealing his face. The demons froze for a moment. Raphaelle flew backwards to the gates. Then she swung with a bow and arrow in her hands. The demons ran out.

She laughed, pivoted, and pointed it at Azrael instead. "Tell me. Why shouldn't I shoot you? Why shouldn't I get even for what you've done to the Khycen?"

"Too late." He shrugged. "The devil's ice."

Raphaelle released the arrow.

Azrael ducked.

The arrow hit the clock.

"Your graces!"

The gatekeepers cried as they watched the missing half of the clock's face materialise in a second, restoring it completely.

Raphaelle slung the bow to her shoulder and glared at them. As soon as they caught her eyes, scarlet tears trickled down their face as they spewed a dark liquid from their mouth before they fell. Then Raphaelle disintegrated into sparks as she neared Thanatos.

"I was never here."

Thanatos bobbed.

When she vanished, three dark armoured sentinels materialised at the arc walkway, taking over the gatekeepers' place.

The clock chimed so loud it blasted the demons' ears.

Metro appeared at the walkway with a scroll, watching the gatekeepers recovering from their injuries. He could only shake his head. One thing he knew of Raphaelle, you'll have to pay the price for her inconvenience. Especially to those who interfere with her plans. Angels and ersatzes alike.

A sentinel to his right coughed.

Metro opened the scroll. "From this day forward, his Highness, Michael, relieve the gatekeepers and her grace Gabrielle of their duty to guard Time." Then he turned to Azrael, who morphed into a human size height while he spread his wings wide. "His highness recognises your grace's endeavour to save the Commander of the Sentinels and Lady Leviel Khycen. Henceforth, he would not pursue your previous lapse in failing to report Shiphrael's life force." The scroll closed. "He also needs you to check on the middle."

"What's his exact wording?"

"We can't have the dead ran amok. Go back to your rightful place, Azrael."

Metro bowed, and he vanished.

18

The Chest

Leviel waited for Talitha to return at the front steps outside their manor's entrance. A pile of pictures from the maze lay beside her. She was scrolling through an image on her laptop when an apricot flower fell on the keyboard. It made her pause and gazed at the nearby garden.

The snow had melted, and the flowers bloomed once more. But a part of Leviel has remained stuck on that ill-fated Christmas night.

After she awoke from the in-between, she was leaning on the willow tree, covered by a red cloak. The red deer lay far from her and transformed into Tiyaniel's figure. He only left her with one sentence: Set her free. Then he vanished. She has not seen him and Haniel ever since. Zeus and Zev were a different story. Then she recalled the time she encountered Tiyaniel's pentagram formation in the ruined manor, revealing her past. Still, she forgot it when she opened her eyes. It only meant a higher angel suppressed Leviel's memory. There could only be one great seraph capable of it—his highness, Samael. It should be his work.

"What are you doing?" asked Talitha, sweaty in her running gear, breaking Leviel's thoughts.

"Remember the statue of 'The Tears of Heaven' from the maze?"

Talitha sat beside her. "Yeah!"

Leviel handed her laptop to her.

"Well, I found another in a blog."

Talitha looked at the laptop's screen, displaying a coloured version of Tears of Heaven. Leviel tried to discern if Shiphrael was seeing it. "I enhanced the woman's angle last night and printed it out." Leviel handed her the picture. "This one is a picture of the little girl we met. Remember, I told you her grandparents deliver vegetables to Mrs Z?"

Talitha scrutinised the picture and then handed it back. "The one I've not met. The girl is a mini version of Aliya Shuruppak."

Leviel gaped. "I came to realise that now. You're right." She forgot her conduit was a cherub and so should resemble the immortal. Leviel searched Aliya on the internet but didn't find any of her images. She wanted to find out if her childhood pictures resembled the cherub. "You're from the House of Shiphrah. Do me a favour and check your side of archives there?"

"Sure. In exchange, you help me find a thing or two."

"No problem." Leviel carried on typing on her laptop.

Talitha went inside in a hurry while Leviel teleported to her room. She slid the chair near the pillar of the house to the side. With a wave, she took the chest from its hiding place. She wiped the dust using her hand, showing an emblem of an oren matching Midael's and a golden scythe. Then she waved her hand, and the chest disappeared.

A thud from Talitha's room made her teleport back to the front steps. Leviel opened her laptop and typed several words. When Talitha came back, she handed Leviel a printout of an emblem.

"This looks familiar," Leviel's brows knitted. She opened her notes. But she knew it was the emblem she saw from the scroll Chamuel lent her in the maze. It was from the book of wisdom and Uriel's crest. Unfortunately, they're forbidden to give Talitha an answer. But it doesn't mean they can't point her in the right direction. "Mayhap, Shiphrah's archive can enlighten us."

"All right, I'll meet you here later," Talitha strode to the gates, appearing late for an appointment.

Leviel bobbed as she watched Talitha walk to her bicycle.

"We're you going?" came Tirzah's voice. Leviel saw her appear in the windows above them.

Talitha paused.

"Shiphrah."

"Oh, okay, never mind. Later, then."

Leviel only glanced at Tirzah before disappearing.

In the next instant, she was in an alley near the House of Adams, and the sky dimmed as she came closer. The mortals vanished as if a barrier cloaked the tower from the rest. When she arrived, the tower's gates swung to the sides. And its main doors slid open. Chamuel stood at the centre.

"You promised her nightmare would stop?"

"Of course," Chamuel stepped out. He had burns on his face. "If she regains her memory, no one will dare covet it."

"It seemed you've learned your lesson the hard way." Leviel eyed the purplish scabs. Chamuel only glared, placed his hands behind his back, and raised his brows. She cleared her throat. "Shiphrah. She'll be at Shiphrah, as you ordered."

Chamuel morphed into a cherub.

"Excellent! And, Leviel?"

"Your grace?"

"Take care," Chamuel vanished.

Leviel's brows knitted as her heart raced. A sudden sound of a horse galloping behind her made her turn. The dark knight from the in-between who took care of the demons appeared. The gatekeepers turned up too.

Leviel felt her blood boil. It struck her now that he and Gabrielle were a team. Not Thanatos. He sent her into a trap. Leviel clamped her hand on her locket while her eyes glowed like gems, staring straight at the gatekeeper standing in front of the dark knight.

The gatekeeper raised his hand, and the scene changed to a barren land covered in snow. Powerful gusts and swirls of dark clouds hovered above them.

"We'll be expecting her grace to join us," said the gatekeeper while a net cast above Leviel. She vanished, but Garash appeared in her place.

Leviel materialised in her Kazi armour behind the gatekeeper while pointing her sword at his neck. "Whether it is you or her grace, take the timepiece if you can."

Dumbfounded, the gatekeepers realise too late their powers weren't working on Leviel. She flew to the knight who charged at her first. Then she whirled to avoid his lance and stepped into the sides as her weapon morphed into a mace before leaping up, giving him a blow onto his head.

The gatekeepers flew after her, only to find they kept teleporting further away from her. They look at the bound immortal and find three kazis with the Selkirk's emblem released him.

"Do you think I'll come here alone?" Leviel asked as she waited for the knight to awoke. Her armband loosened but still covered her tattoo.

The whirlpool of clouds changed into swirls of doves and sailed down, morphing into a golden porcelain angel, freezing everyone but her and the knight.

"Your grace." Leviel faced the archangel, Gabrielle. And on one bended knee, Leviel bobbed her head and then stood. Her pendant disintegrated like ashes in the air while the dark knight darted its lance, emitting a golden force to the ground, sealing the Selkirks in place.

Gabrielle gave her a once over. "Heartbreaker. The chest, if you please."

Leviel darted her eyes to Garash, still frozen.

"I can assure you. It's just you and I."

"But, your grace, are you sure you want it?"

Gabrielle plastered a smile that didn't reach her eyes. "The heavenly commander has figured it out. It was I who was after it."

Leviel nodded. Then the chest appeared.

Gabrielle opened her palms, and it flew to her hand, while a key materialised in her fingers. It shot into the lock, and the chest opened. Inside was a golden leaf laid above a Kazi armour emitting dark energy. The name written on the leaf wasn't Talitha. It was Leviel Khycen.

"What is the—where's Talitha's soul?"

"I'm afraid you've been played. All of us."

A ruby-coloured stone from the Legionary warrior's sword surfaced. It rose to their eye level, emitting dark electric sparks.

Hordes of dove feather ice-blades wrapped around it before it could hit anyone, but Gabrielle's hold on the chest broke, spilling its contents. Then a behemoth reptile emerged. It sprung its tongue to her before she could teleport off.

The golden leaf morphed into golden moths and sailed to Leviel's forehead, while the armour covered her before the stone sailed to her palms. Then, with lightning speed, she sliced the gatekeepers. She removed the Selkirk from the dark knight's control.

Gabrielle tried to use her powers to morph into doves, but the monster wrapped its tongue around her. An ice burgh cut its tongue, releasing her. The clouds turned to a riot of purple while blue lightning rumbled over the welkin, disrupting the archangel.

"She'll rise in a matter of minutes," said Leviel, addressing Gabrielle.

With a wave of Gabrielle's hand, frost cloaked everyone but Leviel and the monster again. It surprised the archangel and fixed her attacks on it. However, it remained unharmed. It captured the dark knight and its horse and swallowed them. Leviel knew it wanted nothing more than the ruby stone. So, she threw it back into the opened trunk. The stone's strong powers broke Gabrielle's hold.

Leviel turned to the ersatzes, freed from the knight's hold. "Go!"

Garash vanished with the Selkirks. In the next second, Coviel and his tail of cherubs appeared. They sailed above Leviel and sprinkled gold dust on her. Then onto the armour.

Its dark energy and her armband vanished. Her exposed tattoo burned, making her wince.

It only meant Raphaelle was immune to the devil's ice. So were her cupids. Leviel stared at the reddish-coloured lights on her palm. She was still her, despite leaving the rock on her body. At least until meeting Samayaja's daughter.

She doesn't know why Raguelle left the stone—perhaps to control both Tiyaniel and Haniel.

"Stop!" Gabrielle shot ice on her legs to keep her rooted. But the monster kept pulling her.

Leviel remained at the sides as she watched Gabrielle struggle with the monster, heedless to the open chest near them. Then it sucked them. Leviel's scalding tattoo disappeared, and the trunk closed.

Sorry. I forgot to remind your grace. The chest was akin to a monster hungry for power.

Wait when I get out of here.

It confirmed that Gabrielle's other forms were unavailable.

No doubt her dominion would detain Leviel if they had enough time.

Only when you're free, your grace. The war is at your doorstep.

The place became the usual scene in the next instant. Mortals passed as if no incident had happened. Leviel teleported a short distance away from the tower gates. The cherubs followed her. From there, she spotted Nathan's walking figure. Then glanced at the balcony where Fenella leaned, lost in her thoughts. She was a girl obsessed with Mattaniah Evander—too much that she dared to sprinkle dirty waters on Talitha. However, Nathan's romantic attachment was superficial. It doesn't mean he doesn't deserve true love.

At the side, Coviel observed Leviel. He understood what she wanted to do. With his command, two cherubs flew high, ready to shoot destiny's arrow. Then Leviel cut the mortal's strings.

"I would endeavour to be a cupid to those I broke their hearts. If there's another life for me."

Coviel nodded, forgetting he was commanding the other cupids. They took it as a signal and released the arrows. They struck their targets while Leviel vanished.

As she teleported, she morphed into her hooded jacket and materialised atop a small hill. She surveyed the passing clouds. The view afforded an illusion that they were within her reach.

Spring came too soon.

She let the last rays of the sun kiss her face, and the chilly wind covered her body. Not long after, the tintinnabulation of church bells from the House of Mikhail increased. So did the thumping of her heart. It was distinguishable from the rest of the tower bells, so strong that its reverberation sent the birds fleeing away from their nest. It meant Michael's strongest proxy, if it weren't himself, arrived.

A sudden blast inside Galen shook the ground, followed by a monstrous fiery winged creature shooting up to the sky, gleaming at the welkin. It appeared as if the sun had risen before it set. Except for one, so closed that Leviel felt the rising temperature multiplied.

The ground Leviel stood crack opened and near threw her off balance. Leviel's sword appeared at once, and she stuck it to the earth as an anchor from the impact while a blue and red glowing light-shielded the tiny lifeless body close to her. Another quake came. It was from the intense energy barrier shielding Galen from the rest of the mortal world.

Shiphrael. Leviel presumed.

"It is done."

It was from the sleeping body on the ground. A small ball of fire sailed and landed atop the body, then disappeared inside it. Soon after, the figure became a beautiful little girl. Several burned wounds materialised on her body.

Leviel stared at the ones on her face.

"A small price. Thanks for lending me the doppelt mode."

Tiny pink sparkling lights rushed from Leviel's hands to the little girl. She crouched and touched the child's wound. It closed, but the scars remained.

Raguelle shook her head.

"This is Shiphrael. Her archers were invisible during the fall because her fire could burn everything in one swoop. You can't heal my wounds."

Leviel dropped her arms.

The cherub struggled to sit and then rubbed her eyes. "I'm curious, if you don't mind. What happened in the in-between?"

Leviel frowned, then shook her head. "I don't understand."

"Both of us know the truth. You and the sentinel cannot be. He's a monster. It was I who made him." Raguelle bit her lower lip. "Young ersatz, you must be kinder to yourself."

"Maybe that's never an option for us ersatz. Like Tiyaniel, he chose the hardest path. And I will not ask why you chose Haniel over Tiyaniel." Leviel squatted. Then gave her a forced smile.

"You angels have your reasons. Anyone outside your kind may never understand."

Raguelle smirked. "Even angels may not."

Leviel's jaw dropped. Then she averted her eyes.

"For a while, I wondered. Why must the monster be someone close to me? As it turns, I changed Haniel's and Tiyaniel's fates. It was my punishment."

A moment passed before Raguelle sighed, breaking their silence.

"It's one way of looking at it. However, all the ersatz who touched that sword died. You didn't. Haniel and Tiyaniel were another exception." Raguelle gazed at the burning sky. "Raphaelle gifted you that armour. It meant she expected more from you. She'd be heartbroken if she didn't know it yet. You betrayed Talitha's trust." Raguelle's fire blazed more than before as her wings spread wide. "You are special, heartbreaker. Just like Midael. Once you see through the past and your bitterness, perhaps you'll be able to appreciate those who love you." Then she vanished.

Leviel kept staring at the yellow petals sailing high before they burned to ashes.

She's special, alright.

It was she who coined the plan to rouse Shiphrael. Her visions were all for her. She looked below to see if a fire was crawling between her legs. Instead, the Seal of Solomon appeared, and Leviel's vision spun.

She appeared in her room at the manor. As she stepped into the corridor, she found the girls hurrying downstairs as several knocks on their main doors echoed in the foyer. When it swung open, her hands fisted at her sides. A black knight greeted Mrs Z. The only contrasting colour on his armour was the silver pauldron where his black coat hung. The golden-red arrow lodged in his chest was intact with its end tail.

Leviel gripped the balustrade.

Heaven's wrath is indeed swift.

With his helmet off, Haniel looked far from his laid-back disposition. His true face was in the open, resembling the silver mask monster from Christmas dawn. But the three red scratched wounds marring his beautiful face were not there. Akin to the burning wounds from the cherub earlier, it won't heal if the doer hasn't forgiven him.

So has she forgiven him?

Leviel scanned the sentinels behind Haniel.

With their helmets on, they were indeed frightening. But not to a Kazi like her, under different circumstances. Ice trickled down her spine as she evaluated her course earlier. Then she looked at Tirzah, Sybil and Dove, huddled behind their manor's steward near out of their wits.

"Apologies for the intrusion, Mrs Z. I need to invite the girls to the council," said Haniel, motioning for his men to get inside.

The girls and Mrs Z backed away. The sentinels grabbed Sybil and Dove.

"W-wait!" Mrs Z tried to pull Haniel's cape, but dropped her hands when an electric bolt ran up her arm.

Leviel let the two knights draw her off the stairs. She tugged her arm, but used little force. They were their equivalent to military police, so she must not use her powers as an ersatz. As the sentinels dragged them out, she saw Mrs Z and Tirzah's helpless faces at the doors, making her head boil.

Useless! Mrs Z didn't make good of her words to take good care of them. Not that there was much she could.

Leviel noticed that as the sentinels walked out of the manor, they divided into two groups. One dragged Sybil and Dove while the other paused outside their gate. Then she saw Haniel approach.

"Where are you taking them?" Leviel asked.

"You should worry more about your fate." Then he placed a hood over her head. "I'll take care of her."

Are you really doing this?

Haniel didn't give the slightest sign that he heard her.

Leviel noticed they turned opposite from where the other group went.

Collywobbles crept as she felt her heart squeeze. Her mission wasn't complete. She didn't want Haniel to sentence her as he did before with Tiyaniel.

"You cannot do this to me! I not only belong to the House of Tobit. I descended from those Raphaelle herself had given life."

Don't I know it, heartbreaker? "Then, where you're heading shouldn't be a problem."

For a second, I thought you had lost your memory.

Leviel screeched at him, contrary to the cool girl she used to be. She reined her hysteria by remembering why she chose this path. Things were easier said than done. To be decisive was one thing, but with its consequence, she was a coward—so different from Tiyaniel. Leviel remembered his last moments under the sentinel's hands.

Oh, how she wished she could be more like him.

Haniel carried on, dragging Leviel into a clearing. As they walked further, Leviel sensed a dozen angels. Their intense energy made her knees quiver. At least they weren't the Galen army for sure.

"Is this she?"

Leviel heard a man's voice right when Haniel's grip tightened, transmitting pain to her shoulder. In reflex, she bit Haniel's hand. The hood over her disappeared, but she didn't let go. However, Haniel only stared. She realised she was biting his gauntlet. So, she unclamped her mouth, forgetting her weak legs, and fell.

Two legionary warriors flanking her stopped her fall.

"Feisty," said Metro, standing before her. He gestured his guards to hold her tightly before turning to Haniel on his left. "I'll return her to you in one piece." In the next instant, one of Metro's men carried her.

"Wait!" Haniel stepped in between them.

Metro shook his head before disappearing into thin air.

The next second, Leviel fell onto her knees and saw a tower's crenellations. Over it, the clouds swirled. She found her hands bound behind her back and saw a lone figure in a golden-red robe standing before her.

"It's been a while, young Leviel." Raphaelle stretched her hand to her.

Epilogue

*L*eviathan clamped his tentacles on Lucifer's body and dragged him deeper into the sea. But the heavy currents reverberated. It was Raphaelle, raging above him. She sent out massive bolts to the surface of the ocean only to return. Raphaelle caught it and swirled, forming a great whirlpool. Before the beast could understand her intent, a powerful force hit him, and he let go of his prey. He sailed several miles away before he recovered.

Peeved, Leviathan went to her straight, only to halt.

Raphaelle's eyes gleamed, while a thick greyish electric volt formed on her palms.

Lucifer awoke from his doldrums just in time. He crossed his arms in front of him and then braced himself. Raphaelle delivered a powerful explosion underwater.

It emptied the sea, but the great pleroma formation remained.

Lucifer and Leviathan staggered as the waters crashed back onto them. While Raphaelle screamed as she pooled more powers into her hands before slamming it at the seal. Another strong turbulence shook the waters, but not enough to open the sea.

In the aftermath, Leviathan stared at Raphaelle. Then back away. He tried his best to stop several of his legs from moving.

I hope she didn't notice me. Should I tell her I was only interested in the serpent? It's what his body wanted.

His thoughts were clear to her. She understood his skittishness. Most creatures knew of her reputation.

"Raphaelle, for our sakes. Quit it," said Lucifer, panting. When their eyes locked, hers gleamed again. He raised his arms. "A break, if you please."

Thousands of bolts plunged into the sea before Raphaelle could decide. It roasted every being it struck.

She summoned her powers while golden electrical volts shrouded her. Then she spread her hands, shielding all the sea creatures.

The explosion on the surface hit her veil as the earth quivered in its wake. Thick soot spread, covering the shallow waters. Raphaelle's electric shield broke at the impact, shoving her deeper into the sea. It ceased a few minutes later.

"Who was that?" Lucifer asked.

"The commander," said Raphaelle. She closed her eyes while her heart ceased to beat.

"And the other?" Lucifer observed the murky water above them.

Raphaelle's heartbeat resumed, and she could breathe in and out. "None that you've met before."

Soon, the heaviness of the water overwhelmed her, and she gave in to fatigue. Raphaelle nodded, and Leviathan wrapped his tentacles around them. The next moment, they left the shallow waters. He brought them deeper into a trench. As they reached it, the water subsided, and they landed on dry sand. Raphaelle noticed a force propelled it to remain above.

Leviathan let go of them near the rocks, careful not to drop them too hard.

Raphaelle wasn't blind to his actions. She and Lucifer crawled to the rock before they sat and leaned on it. They both released a long sigh. Then their eyes opened.

A child was where Leviathan stood. She scanned for him and found Lucifer's fluttering eyes.

"A child?" Raphaelle straightened her back. They had been fighting him for several hours and didn't even know they were fighting a youngster.

"I could morph in my actual form, but only in this place." *Sadly, there was none to witness it until now.* Leviathan thought, but didn't dare voice it.

Raphaelle read his mind. "You're a child?"

"We heard you the first time," said Lucifer. "Such a disgrace, eh?"

"Indeed. For you and I." Raphaelle gave him a stern look. It meant none of them could say they bullied a kid.

"At least I'm younger than you," Lucifer averted his face. Raphaelle knew then he would never keep it to himself.

"I've always been a child," said Leviathan, halting their bickering.

Raphaelle shook her head while Lucifer still observed him with a heavy heart. "What did you do?"

"When I was a cherub, I excelled and stood out. Our leader once asked who was the bravest among us all. I was foolish and said I. The next thing I knew, I ended up trapped in this body. I regretted it. But what can regret do? It can't change anything, can't it? Then hatred consumed me. I grew into my beast form and lost my angelic powers. I could never morph back outside of this cove since then."

Raphaelle nodded and turned to Lucifer. She wanted to berate him, but realised he was out of it.

Locked in his thoughts, Lucifer stared at Leviathan for a long time. "Is it just me, or do you also think he looks a tad familiar?"

Raphaelle gave him a side glance. "He reminds me of you."

"I'm serious!" Lucifer narrowed his eyes at her. She glared back. Raphaelle does not understand what he's getting at. Leviathan walked over to them and sat. She saw expectation and a bit of awe on his face as he gazed at Lucifer.

"What is going on up there?" Leviathan asked. "Are you rebelling again?"

Raphaelle could not help but burst out laughing. The child was innocent. It had the guts to ask Lucifer, the dark prince himself. Well, if word gets out she bullied a kid, this one would be her perfect return.

Lucifer's face and ears turned red to Raphaelle's surprise. *Oh, the brat knows how to be embarrassed. It was a first.*

"When did I stop? Rebelling, I mean," said Lucifer, daring the kid to say more.

Raphaelle clobbered Lucifer's head.

"Ow!" Lucifer rubbed his injury. "Now that I think about it, it made no difference. Whether you or Michael raise the nursling, they'll be on a tight rein. You have a heavy hand. Heavier than Michael, perhaps."

It earned him a couple of thwacks. "I never laid my hand on you when you were little. I should've."

Amazed that Lucifer didn't hit back, Leviathan looked at Raphaelle with regard.

She noticed his bewilderment and pointed at Lucifer. "You should ask how he escaped?"

Lucifer cringed. "I didn't. It's more like someone freed me. By the by, the abyss dried out. It's colder than the tropics now."

Raphaelle massaged the side of her temples. "It must be Shiphrael."

"Oh, you mean the mortal? What did you do to her?"

Raphaelle grabbed his shoulders. "You can't wash your hands off of this." Lucifer's face paled. She dropped her arms, but it needed to be said. "If you'd only stayed below, then none of this would happen. If only you remained the Lucifer—"

"You could have spoken for us. You knew us best."

She felt as if he had stabbed her. He didn't shout, but it was all the same to her. Raphaelle gritted her teeth, "Past being the operative word here."

"And the arrows?"

Raphaelle grimaced. She knew it'd come up. "I was a coward. You know how the cadre works."

Lucifer stared into her eyes. "I know the cadre has Michael. You wouldn't be out of favour if you spoke up. You didn't want to. It's because of Gabrielle, right?" Even if her life depended on it, Raphaelle wouldn't admit it. So she averted her eyes while he was in his tirade. "Well, at least Midael and Shiphrael did their best to stop me from destroying myself at the expense of defying Michael. It can't be said for you." Then he scooted farther from her.

At a different time, Raphaelle will find him amusing. She fisted her hands, summoning patience, but lost. "At least you're aware."

"Oh, I'm well aware of the irony of it all. Our love's fate lies in your hands—the archangel who had never felt it."

Raphaelle couldn't take it and shoved him.

He didn't budge. It made Raphaelle stew more. Leviathan, on the side, kept swinging his head at both of them.

"I heard the first couple you matched, an angel and ersatz, was a complete disaster. They ended up killing each other." Lucifer cracked up.

Any angel would earn a blow on their head for this comment. They knew nothing irritated her more than the remark of that tragic day. Raphaelle gnawed her teeth and then relaxed. It was Lucifer. As his teacher, he expected more from her than anyone. So, she'll give him this. After all, she didn't help him.

He paused, noticing her quietness. "They don't know, do they?"

"Samyaja's daughter is a headache. Don't change the subject. Are you telling me I don't know what love is?"

"Do you? I bet you don't know how easily it can turn to hate. I've witnessed it. Give or take a thousand-fold. Maybe more. Though not so much for the reverse."

It appears he and the father shared the same belief in love. So, she had to draw blood where she should. "Look at you."

"Look at Gabrielle."

Dammit! Raphaelle bit her tongue. Perhaps it was not the havoc he'll cause she dreaded the most when he's out but his jabs.

Leviathan kept rubbing his neck as he swung from her to Lucifer and back. Raphaelle sent invisible energy to ease the tension on his neck and shoulders. It's the least she could do.

"What about Gabrielle?" Leviathan asked, leaning his head in his hand.

Raphaelle glared.

"Never mind."

Lucifer's laughter turned to roars. Then he noticed the sand's colour was gold. He built a sandcastle using his powers and then used his legs to destroy it. He constructed yet another. For a moment, silence reigned. Raphaelle busied herself feeding the fishes passing by.

"Why haven't Gabrielle's bitterness turned to love? You've never done it. Have you?"

Raphaelle closed her eyes. *There he goes again on Gabrielle.* If she hadn't known things would get worse, she'd have the two strung together.

"There are outside forces that stop—"

"You're not the master of the red arrows. You only do your best as a soldier."

Raphaelle raised her hand to smack Lucifer again but stopped mid-way. She cannot tell him more than what she should.

"The mortal realm isn't a happy place, is it? And no," he clamped a hand on her mouth. "Not because of me. Don't blame it all on me. I alone am not responsible. Your cupids have made havoc with it, too."

Raphaelle removed his hand. "The wedding aside, I have always excelled in my responsibilities. I can assure you I can turn hate to love."

"You can try. But you'll never succeed on Miss Heartbreaker. Leviel, is it?"

Raphaelle blanched.

Haniel and Leviel's affair and Gabrielle were her imperfection.

Meanwhile, Leviathan yawned. Lucifer pointed at him and gestured for them to lower their voices. She nodded. She watched as he reached out a hand to touch Leviathan's forehead, but withdrew.

Lucifer destroyed his castle again.

"Without sarcasm this time. What do you know about Gabrielle's plan?"

A small canister appeared in Raphaelle's hand, and she took a swig. Good. They're back to business. One thing she gathered, he didn't know the entire situation in the capital.

"The immortals had never severed their alliance with the Grigoris. Yet, they've grown in numbers." Then Raphaelle lowered her voice even more. "Was it negligence or deliberate? I do not know."

"Because you can't question it either way. Sorry, I just got out of prison. I can't help you. I haven't had time to mingle."

"Even if you do, you won't help."

Silence was her only answer.

Raphaelle took a deep breath. "Fear blinds her."

Lucifer's jaw dropped before recovering. "Fear? For whom? No matter who it is, she has you."

Raphaelle lowered her head, avoiding his eyes. She knew she added the last bit to lighten up her friend's case.

"Shiphrael."

"Then there's your answer."

Many loved the eighth, yet no one could save her from her fate. What more for Gabrielle? Those who love Shiphrael wouldn't give up.

Leviathan got up.

"You're messing everything because you have the freedom. Look at me. I'm here down underwater. The other aquatic creature doesn't come near me. Afraid I would bite—"

"You do bite." Lucifer winked.

Leviathan scowled before continuing, "None of them knew I don't need to feed. I have space, and so do they. My life is peaceful. Too peaceful."

His criticism didn't sit well with Raphaelle, who kicked the pebbles near her. "Yes, we are indeed aggravating circumstances. It's too late to undo it."

"Is it? Well, we share the same sentimentality about regrets. I know that if you can't undo it, it's better not to dwell on it. You'll only make it worst. Perhaps it is for the best." Leviathan clapped his hands. "It appears my patience had paid off since I have the two of you as my company."

It was akin to splashing them with cold water.

Raphaelle bit back her riposte while she gave him a once-over. Arguing with a child makes her one. Then she paused. He reminded her of the person who feigned his defiance before her fall with Lucifer into the waters.

"What is he talking about?" Lucifer asked, letting the emerald pebbles float and shoot above the water and finding it interesting that not a single drop spilt on the cove.

"The Pleroma." Raphaelle frowned at the waters above them.

"Well, on that matter, I think they're discarding you. How about—"

"Don't you dare offer me a partnership in your rebellion?"

Lucifer hid his grin. "You can think about it. As—"

He stopped. Two pairs of eyes awaited him to continue, but he did not.

Raphaelle tried to discern what was going on with him. *Is someone reaching out to him? Who has enough power to reach them below there?*

She flicked her hand. "Oi!"

"Sorry for dazing out. My body needed to adjust to being on the surface. Well—then back." Lucifer observed the fishes above, looking less interested in Raphaelle. "I thought no fish could dwell on this bottom-most?"

He lies.

Raphaelle's face darkened.

"I'm the source of the oxygen." Leviathan beamed at Lucifer. He felt rather proud of it.

Lucifer kept nodding at whatever Leviathan said.

"If you're interested later, we can visit and observe some—or not." He sensed Lucifer's mind was somewhere else. "Take some rest." Depleted from fighting them, Leviathan fell asleep. This time for real.

When he kept to himself, Raphaelle sat closer to Lucifer. "Both commanders send their regards and welcome you with open arms."

Lucifer nodded and then paused, seeing her keen eyes. He fell on his back, destroying his castle. "That is utter nonsense."

"For a minute, I thought hell shaped you into a sheep."

Raphaelle scooted farther from him and settled across the child. She leaned at the rock before closing her eyes. Then opening them again and observed Leviathan. She fell into a slumber, looking at the child's peaceful face.

A sudden sound of splashing roused Raphaelle. Her heart pounded, and she surveyed the place. Lucifer was nowhere in sight, and so was Leviathan. She scrambled to her feet, sailed back into the water, and met Leviathan in his beast form. She could sense his anger as he shot his tentacles in a swift. Raphaelle's shield took the blow, shoving him a few paces.

"Why are you leaving me?"

"Where is Lucifer?" asked Raphaelle without a care for his outburst.

"He promised he would let you stay! You can't leave."

"I have no time for your fits."

Before she could summon her powers, Leviathan had his tentacles wrapped around her. Raphaelle had not recovered in full and soon choked. She was trying not to lose consciousness when a dark figure came. Then fire wrapped around Leviathan, forcing him to let go of her.

Raphaelle found two arms wrapped around her, pulling her to the surface. Gone was the pleroma that locked the Baltic Sea.

"Stop! Don't go!"

Leviathan was on their heels, but they soared higher and out of his reach.

"The father heard your calling. I promised I would visit you," said Uriel, with his golden bare chest in the open. Raphaelle found her bearing and scrambled out of his arms. The great cherubim gave her a side glance before sailing down. "I am Uriel, and I give you my word."

Leviathan looked with longing but obeyed and dived back. They waited until his shadow disappeared. When only the white foam from the waves remained, they sailed down closer to the water.

"You always have a way of diplomacy."

She thought a fight would need to break before Leviathan calmed.

Uriel grinned from ear to ear. "I wasn't lying either."

She doesn't doubt it. Uriel never lies. Good thing the burns he got from Michael's punishment healed now.

"Were you spying on us?"

Uriel put some distance between them.

"I was monitoring Lucifer."

"Where is he?" Raphaelle gave him a stern look. Then she searched and whirled around, hoping to spot Lucifer.

"I take it this is your show of gratitude. You're welcome anyhow. And as for the brat, it's a long story." He morphed into his beast-like angelic form with a lion's face. Uriel soared above her.

My dear Raphaelle. I never thought you were so unkind as to turn that cherub into Leviathan. Lucifer's voice echoed in her head. Did you know why Gabrielle almost killed Midael when we were young?

How can I forget? What's the connection?

He is the only one who can beat her. And mark my words, he will.

"Ignore him," said Uriel, back to her side.

His bare chest distracted Raphaelle, and she turned away from him. "Lucifer, come and explain things!"

Better find love, my dear General.

Raphaelle turned to Uriel with hands on her hips. "What is going on? And no, don't tell me it's a long story!".

Uriel morphed into his human figure, extending the moment. Then he released a sigh.

"Gabrielle allowed the experiments on the Nephilim."

Raphaelle fell, but soared back before she could hit the water. This time, she felt drained. "They were to be killed. Not—"

"Exploited?"

Raphaelle froze. She read the truth in his eyes.

"COME," came a deep voice. It reverberated on the welkin.

Both archangels turned serious and spread their wings wide, submitting immediately.

"Leviathan would have to wait," said Uriel. He wanted nothing more than to escape Raphaelle's interrogation. Not that he would run from it.

"Indeed."

"You always want the last word."

"Like you aren't?"

It made him smile. But there was no end to it unless he gave in.

Uriel vanished.

Raphaelle materialised in a top twenty-story building behind a tiny toddler's figure wearing a white robe. The cherub stared at the darkened sky with a fiery ball at the centre. He was holding the same ball in his left hand.

"Come on. I've got no time to dally." The toddler waved his hand to have her come closer.

Raphaelle trembled and promised to be merciful if she survived the ordeal. She knelt and bowed low.

"Five per cent. That is my quota." Then she handed a scroll.

"Five per cent! Remind me, who started a wager with me, proud and resolute that love was what it all takes to save this world? You even took on Uriel's bait." The cherub grunted and then threw the scroll back to her. "Your numbers don't reflect you."

Another angel in a red robe appeared and, like Raphaelle, couldn't stop himself from shaking. He bent to his knees, bowed, and handed the scroll to the toddler.

"Your numbers had increased by three-fold."

Azrael kept his head bent.

"This world is still promising if both of you switched your numbers." The toddler stared at their heads, then averted his eyes at the raging fire. "It has begun." Without preamble, he jumped off the building, morphing into hundreds of canaries.

When they were sure he wasn't coming back, Raphaelle turned to Azrael. "You could have just lowered your numbers. Then mine would have increased."

"It's beyond my means. They wanted to die. So, they did," said Azrael, releasing a long breath he was holding in.

"We need to work with each other."

"Love is a contributing force driving mortals to death." Azrael crossed his arms.

Raphaelle frowned. "And what's on the top?"

"Ignorance."

The archangels burst out laughing. Raphaelle was the first to recover and stirred Azrael back. "Then we need everyone in this."

Behind them, a whirl of fire and ash weaved into one, morphing into Uriel. "Is this about Lucifer? You should just let it go. After all, you lost beautifully."

"You're late! And be serious for once!" Raphaelle pouted, then jerked back to Azrael. "We have to do it. Otherwise, we'll never get the father back."

Uriel and Azrael could only stare at her. Their father, great as he may be, had changed since the fall. And for the worst.

"Uriel, come over," said Samael, who pointed at Shiphrael's ball of fire.

"You know, we risk having everything fall into pieces," Azrael said, as it was. A fact.

Raphaelle bobbed. "It will be. In the end."

"They will never work together. Unless—" Azrael gestured to the heavenly commanders chatting with Uriel. Raphaelle glanced at them. He came closer to her and hunched at her ear. "Unless you put that brat in the equation."

"You and I will be toasted if that happens." Raphaelle jerked her head, bumping Azrael's. He vanished before her and then appeared.

"My point, exactly."

A tintinnabulation reverberated while the figure at the right corner burst into dozens of canneries surrounded by blue light before it disappeared.

Relief washed over Azrael and Raphaelle. They were on their toes when their commander, Michael, was near. Now that he's away, the pain in their neck lightened.

A crow flew past them and multiplied while the great seraph's form disintegrated.

"Well, if you want your plan to work, you better ask for his support. Now is the best time. Don't stare at me with puppy eyes. I'm not going near that being." Azrael hid behind Raphaelle, finding the fiery figure watching them.

"He doesn't bite," said Raphaelle, more to herself.

"Good luck with that."

"It's now or never." Raphaelle fisted as she dashed in front of Samael, stood at attention, and bobbed. "Sire, we have a proposal."

What do you mean we? Count me out, said Azrael in her head.

Samael remained silent.

Raphaelle's mind scrambled to think. *How do you ask someone for help, knowing he'll lose everything in the end? If it works.*

Samael looked at the burning ball. Then back to Raphaelle. "I give you leave to speak your mind as long as you keep it short."

She was not stupid. "We need you to tip the balance."

Samael gave her a lopsided grin before turning to give her his complete attention.

Oh shit! Here comes no turning back. Raphaelle felt her body covered in ice.

"Which side?" asked Samael.

"The other side."

Acknowledgement

This year didn't start well for me. Fatigue was always in the way of my writing. So, I appreciate those who held my hand throughout the process of finishing Leviel's story. I want to thank auntie Maria and uncle Sean for, without their continued support, I would have given up a long time ago. I want to thank my dear brother, John, for always being there. Lastly, Bryan, and Ben, whose continued encouragement inspired me to write more.

Author's Note

Leviel and Haniel's story continues in Book 2 of the series. Although the side stories may be redundant with Book 1, they are different. It brings more clarity to the whole plot of the series.

As revealed here, Michael has three proxies: the priest, Mattaniah and Midael. If you've read Book 1, you might have figured the priest is Oscar de la Luz. More of his character will be in Midael's story.

When I wrote this book, I started writing after Shiphrael's awakening. But then I figure it'll be hard for readers to follow and may be repeated in Midael's story. So that wasn't part of this book. On that, Leviel and Haniel had a happy ending. I was glad this book didn't follow that direction because it made me love Leviel and Haniel.

About the Author

Alegna Eiram is a reverse of the author's first name, **Angela Marie Cariaga**. She has a bachelor's degree in Biology-Zoology and dropped out of Medicine. She is a Roman Catholic. She recently wrote The Irony of True Love Shiphrael, House of Mikhail, the first book in the series.

www.ingramcontent.com/pod-product-compliance
Lightning Source LLC
Chambersburg PA
CBHW020335160726
47992CB00004B/1850